Joshua Hatton

Throughout the Year

Poems old and new

Joshua Hatton

Throughout the Year
Poems old and new

ISBN/EAN: 9783337212759

Printed in Europe, USA, Canada, Australia, Japan

Cover: Foto ©Andreas Hilbeck / pixelio.de

More available books at **www.hansebooks.com**

THROUGHOUT THE YEAR.

Poems Old and New.

BY

GUY ROSLYN,

LONDON :

W. B. WHITTINGHAM & CO.,

91, GRACECHURCH STREET, E.C.

—

1886.

W. B. WHITTINGHAM & CO.,

PRINTERS,

91, GRACECHURCH STREET, LONDON,

AND

"THE CHARTERHOUSE PRESS,"

44, CHARTERHOUSE SQUARE, E.C.

SOME OF THE FOLLOWING POEMS HAVE APPEARED IN—ALL THE YEAR ROUND, BELGRAVIA, CASSELL'S MAGAZINE, CHAMBERS'S JOURNAL, COLBURN'S NEW MONTHLY, THE GENTLEMAN'S MAGAZINE, THE GRAPHIC, ST. JAMES'S MAGAZINE, LEISURE HOUR, LONDON SOCIETY, ONCE A WEEK, THE PICTORIAL WORLD, THE QUIVER, TINSLEY'S MAGAZINE, TEMPLE BAR, THE VICTORIA MAGAZINE, WARNE'S INTERNATIONAL ANNUAL, AND OTHER PUBLICATIONS.

TO

THE MEMORY OF

MY WIFE

THIS BOOK IS INSCRIBED.

CONTENTS.

	PAGE
When Wheat is Green.	1
From Winter to Spring	3
A Night in March.	4
Old Bells	5
Two Names on a Tree	7
An Old Village	9
An April Daisy	12
A Star of Hope	14
New Days.	16
The Wind in the City	17
Songs of Spring	19
Hope and Faith	20
Messengers in May	22
Looking for Love	24
A May Song	26
Dusk	27
I Love you Best	28
Blossoming	30
Do Not Forget	32
Spring	34
Above Douglas Bay	35
In Eden.	38
An Invitation	39

	PAGE
True Words, ...	41
Evening . .	43
The Pilot's Girl .	44
The Question . . .	46
In a Meadow	48
A Day in June . .	49
Sunday Morning .	51
Under a Tree . .	53
Birds in the Wood	55
Summer Eves . . .	57
Summer of Content . .	59
Old Love and New . . .	61
The Silent Thrush	63
Birds	66
The Signal	68
Mary	70
A Rest by the Way . .	72
A Dream of a Dream . .	74
Totter Bells .	76
Betrothal . .	78
In the Cool of the Day	80
Marriage Morn . . .	82
While the Sun Goes Down	84
Aftermath .	86
Jilted	87
The Last Days of Summer	89
Watching for Sails	91

A Quiet Night 93

A Season-Ring 95

Waiting 97

Autumn Voices 99

In the Bay 100

At the Fifth Act 103

By the Orchard Wall 106

An Old Picture 108

Changing Pictures . 110

Ruined 113

Waiting for Escort 115

Summer's Wraith . . 119

Autumn Rain 121

Waiting for Winter . . . 123

Not for Love 125

Bridal Bells 127

When the Wind Blows 129

The Bretby Bells 131

Winter Weather 135

A Beggar Man 136

A Winter Night 138

Abel Kare 139

Sigh not So . . . 142

The Coming of the Snow . . 144

Burnt Wings . . . 146

Poverty's Winter 148

Je Vous Adore . . . 149

	PAGE
THE FIRST SNOWFALL	151
DEAD DAYS	153
WINTER WALKS	155
MY LADY'S FAVOURS	156
ON THE HILL	158
ENCHANTED EMBERS	159
BY THE HEARTH	163
HOW LONG?	165
A WHITE WOOD	167
THE GARDEN SEAT	169
A DECEMBER DAISY	171
PICTURES ON THE PANES	174
SIMPLICITY	176
WHILE THE SNOW FALLS	178
THE LADY OF BLACK FRIARS	181
WE WILL HOLD OUR OWN	185
CHASTELARD TO MARY STUART	187
THE FREE SWORD	191
WRITTEN IN BLOOD	193
LOVE'S HARVEST	195
THE BETTER CHRISTMAS	197
ZEPHADEE	200
WILDERMERE	207
EDGAR	213

THROUGHOUT THE YEAR.

WHEN WHEAT IS GREEN.

WHEN wheat is green in furrowed fields,
  And forest lanes are lined with leaves,
And passion unto pleading yields,
  And ev'ry mateless maiden grieves
For lack of love—at such a time
My pleasure will be in its prime.

The clouds that keep away the sun,
  And cover up the moon at night,
Before the strong March wind will run,
  And leave the heavens blue and bright ;
The sun will shine upon the sea—
The moon will light the wood for me,

B

And then, ah then ! O dearest days !
  Laburnum branches, thick with bloom,
Will throw their gold on garden ways,
  And kiss the windows of my room ;
And then the day !   How will it be
To live in such felicity ?

My brow with blossoms will be bound,
  And from my fears I shall be free :
O tardy Time, bring quickly round
  The merriest month of all for me !
That I may hear the church boys sing,
And on my finger see the ring !

FROM WINTER TO SPRING.

I.

AT last the baffled snow slips from the roof,
Before the mild persisting of the rain;
And in the east, keeping all doubt aloof,
Are streaks of spring-foretelling gold again.

And soon warm-coming winds will swing the gull,
And sway the old boat gently in the bay;
And once again the great trees will be full
Of leaves and birds, to charm the length'ning
day.

II.

After the winter snow,
After the joyless days,
Green things in hedges grow,
And kingcups blow
In old familiar ways,
After the winter snow.

After the dreary days,
After the sleety rain,
Hope walks about our ways,
With cheering lays,
And bids us smile again
After the dreary days.

A NIGHT IN MARCH.

In this March night
Grey Winter murmurs in the gloom,
With sad foreknowledge of his doom :
His robes are draggled through the land—
The sceptre withers in his hand ;
And from the west the strong young Spring
Flies hitherward on coloured wing.

This mild March night
The crocus pushes through the sod—
The golden miracle of God !
And sap in old trees, damp and drear,
Makes song we are too gross to hear,
To thrill the branches into green,
Wherein young birds will sing unseen.

OLD BELLS.

AFTER years of city toil I hear the village bells ;
They sing a new song while the old song in my
    mem'ry dwells—
A strange new song, with strange new words that
    many sorrows bring ;
O would that I could hear again the song they
    used to sing
When I was young, and love was young, and the
    green sod's daisy stud
Was a sweet new thing that won the heart, and
    hope was in the bud !
Ring on, old bells ! sing on, sweet bells ! ring on !
    for now I hear
The echo of lost melodies, and distant days seem
    near.

Day is dying, the lake has lost the light of after-
    noon ;
Stars shine, and waters shimmer round the shadow
    of the moon :

Missing Page

I knew not anything of gloom,
 I scarce could happier be;
But autumn came, and came again,
 And changed to winter strife,
And I have drunk the last sweet drain
 From out the cup of life.

I tried to think him in the right,
 But scorn came up instead—
How should I know that in the fight
 My love had long been dead?
And now, alas! I can but plead
 That strength may come to me,
That I may only once more read
 The two names on the tree.

AN OLD VILLAGE.

OLD village, what potent league have you made
   With Time and with Progress that you are free
From the show of change, and are still arrayed
   In the dress of an ancient century ?
Where is, snorting Steam with his busy wheels ?
   He mixes no note with your singing stream :
You are as fair as a vision that steals
   From Memory's house in a pleasant dream.

Under the hill is the lordly demesne,
   And amidst the great trees the old spires rear ;
And the thick manor walls are high, and green
   With the growth of many a peaceful year :
There lord after lord has ruled in his pride,
   At banquets attended by clown and page,
To honour a daughter robed as a bride,
   Or a son and heir at the coming of age.

The village shoemaker sits with his thread,
   And thinks and thinks with a serious look ;
There may be a half-made rhyme in his head,
   For he works all day near a singing brook ;

Or he may be deep in affairs of State,
  Rehearsing a cry for a new crusade ;
Or affairs of love, and the unkind fate—
  Of a ring that for him was never made.

*   *   *   *   *   *

How idly goes the cottage smoke aloof
  In thin blue wreaths that strive to kiss cool
    leaves,
And throw their shadows on the sunny roof,
  Where stately pigeons strut about the eaves
And watch the curled-up cat upon the wall,
  And wonder if she be indeed asleep ;
Or look into the garden ground, where all
  The sweet old-fashioned flow'rs grow in a heap.

How many things around are fair to see !
  How many voices that are sweet to hear !
How many customs quaint and old there be,
  For grave observance through the quiet year !
Here weather-saws, that have some truth, are told,
  To guide the men who work upon the farm ;
And signs are sought foretelling heat or cold,
  And what will prosper and what come to harm.

Here is a green, with seats around great trees,
  Where th' old folk sat when they were girls and
    boys;
And where at evening they still take their ease,
  Rememb'ring in their children youthful joys;
Passing this way men may forget their grief,
  For who could here let thoughts run into gloom?
With every little straggling lane in leaf?
  And every little cottage porch in bloom?

AN APRIL DAISY.

WHITE daisy in the growing grass,
  Now I have lost my winter fear—
  Pure promise of the budding year,
And pleasures that shall come to pass.

  Of summer and the sun you speak,
Of childhood with its healthy cheek,
Red-ripening lips and sweet glad eyes,
Where truest love untainted lies,
Where beauty laughs, and passion shows
Its colour like an opening rose.

  Pink-lidded harbinger of spring !
You tell of swallows on the wing—
Swallows that are ever roaming,
Sailing, sinking in the gloaming,
And dipping in the silver stream,
Upon whose banks young lovers dream
In dim seclusion ; where the beech
Bends over with a graceful reach

Unto the water's shelving brim ;
Where swarms of shining minnows swim,
And glide among tall taper reeds,
And under waving folds of weeds.
You speak of blue-bells in the wood,
Of fruitfulness and fairyhood.
The lady smocks with faint blush stain
Shall line the brown paths of the lane ;
The butterflies and spring-time noise
Shall bless the hearts of merry boys,
And western winds shall smooth the curls
That shade the eyes of happy girls.

Gold-crested herald of the spring !
You tell of blackbirds that shall sing
In secret plots of freshened green ;
Of walks in evening dusk, between
The sinking sun and rising moon,
When trees are full of leaves in June.

White daisy in the growing grass,
Now I have lost my winter fear—
Pure promise of the budding year,
And pleasures that shall come to pass.

A STAR OF HOPE.

A STAR above the steeple-top,
   In twilight but a feeble spark,
Is hanging as the shadows drop,
   And brighter burns as comes the dark.

Let not your courage from you go
   When common troubles drag you down ;
Your face that now is white for woe,
   With sunny joy may yet be brown.

Be pure in heart, in peace or pain ;
   Obey the still small voice that calls :
The star above the steeple-vane
   Shines stronger as the darkness falls.

Hope, like a diamond in the coal,
   Shall shine, however black the night :
Keep well your eyes unto the goal,
   And do not tire, but trust and fight.

Because the path has led your feet
  To places bleak and bare with blight,
Seek not for safety in retreat ;
  Still forward go and look for light.

And if in vain you seek a ray
  Of sun to break the clouds of sorrow,
Still fight it out—work well to-day,
  And do not fear about to-morrow.

NEW DAYS.

O FRESH and fair young leaves of spring!
What shall I do but weep or sing?
In gratitude for brighter life,
You promise after winter strife;
And for all pleasures that you bring,
O fair and fresh young leaves of spring!

O new and sweet birds of the spring!
That through the long warm days will sing;
I would that you could know how dear
You are to me that give you fear—
Could know my thanks for joys you bring,
O sweet and new birds of the spring!

O gentle spirit of the spring!
Breathing in each new living thing;
I would that I to thee might raise
In thankfulness some fitting praise;
But for all blessings that you bring
My words are weak, O gentle Spring!

THE WIND IN THE CITY.

THE wind is in the city; he is come from the
    wintry main,
To wrestle with stony steeples, and to make us
    think again
Of some we love who have gone down to the
    mighty sea in ships,
And whose cheeks a little while ago were lifted to
    our lips;
O may they all be safely steered from the hidden
    granite's grips!

The lamps along the gusty streets flicker in fear
    and sputter;
And men are caught at the corners and pushed
    into the gutter;
Tiles are wrenched away from the roofs, and about
    their heads are thrown,
And out of every passage comes a mysterious
    moan;
And the alehouse signboards squeak on their rusty
    hinges and groan.

The bells that strike the hour seem near, and
  then they seem far away;
The wind is blowing about the noise, and all
  sounds are astray;
They cling to roofs, like restless ghosts, and then
  rush to the river,
Where waters under doubtful lights about the
  barges quiver,
And 'neath the great storm's flapping wings the
  bridges rock and shiver.

The wind has turned from his anger to sing a
  song of pity,
As he leaves the streets and spires of the
  startled, shaken city;
In a little while he is far off, and quiet as a rill
That runs below tall sheltering trees around a
  forest hill;
And ev'ry little cottage now below the stars is
  still.

SONGS OF SPRING.

WHEN will the songs be old that tell of spring?
Of buttercups that blow and birds that sing?
Ah, never may my losses or my gains
Make common things to me of fields and lanes!

When I behold the springtime sunbeams fall,
And light the chilly moss upon the wall,
May I be moved to think of hedges green—
Of lilac with laburnum boughs between:

Of clouds in starlight and of changing moons—
Of shiny, breezy morns and idle noons—
Of paths o'ergrown, where stray wind sing to
    streams
The sweet songs of our youngest, dearest dreams.

Now I remember many a pleasant rhyme,
Born of the joy that comes in budding time;
And made for love in simple days of ease,
When mortals had more leisure for the trees.

When will the songs be old that always bring,
In wildest days, some music of the spring;
And make us smile to think what will be soon,
When garden roses breathe below the moon?

HOPE AND FAITH.

In spring I went into the wood,
And smiling Hope before me stood ;
She sang to me for one long morn
Of present love and joys unborn :
It was an easy, pleasant thing
To walk the wood with Hope in spring.

The wood in winter was not fair ;
I walked therein ; Hope was not there ;
At length I called upon her name,
And looked around, but no one came :
Then darkness came with chilling rain,
And for the path I groped in vain.

For hours I felt about the trees,
Until I sank upon my knees,
For I was weak and did not know
What thing to think, which way to go ;
And then I saw a strange light shine,
And some one's hand took hold of mine.

Then I was guided to the town,
And on my knees again went down
For thanks, " Dear Hope, what shall I say .
For bringing me into the way ?"
Then, with a gentle voice, she saith,
" I am not Hope ; my name is Faith."

MESSENGERS IN MAY.

AGAIN we have the young Spring,
When linnets sing and larks sing.
Many timid flowers are seen
Shud'ring in the new chill green.
Hearts be merry ! Winter sorrow
Shall be dead upon the morrow.

The sun show'rs, and the colour'd bow
Of promise, and the stars also,
The green sea, and the yellow sand,
The moving leaves, the painted land,
Will give new life, and Hope's sweet wine
That makes a mortal half divine.
Day is conquering the night,
And blossom covering the blight.

Many poets gone away
Have sung of Spring's delicious day ;
And many poets will sing again
Of gardens after summer rain—

Of water in the noonday blaze,
Of early morning's faery haze,
Of evening when the swallows fly
Under misty-coloured sky,
Over brooks where pinkies swim
Round the water lily's rim.

Now the spring-time is a-coming
With its ditty, drone, and humming ;
With the nightingale and thrush,
And the perfume of the bush ;
With the moth and burnish'd bees,
And the music of the trees ;
And with happiest, merriest din,
Spring-time is a-coming in.

LOOKING FOR LOVE.

As a fisherman looks out over the bay
   For a ship that comes from sea,
I look for my love from day to day,
   But my love comes not to me.

Who is the maid that the finger of fate
   Has given, and where lives she ?
How long shall I linger, and hope, and wait,
   Before she will come to me ?

Or have I no love, and shall I be blown
   Like a lost boat out to sea ?
No, pleasure and peace shall be my own,
   And my love shall come to me.

And when and where shall I know my sweet doom,
   Indoors or where flowers grow ?
Will the pear trees all be white with bloom,
   Or will they be white with snow ?

Have I ever heard of your name in talk?
Or seen you a child at play?
Are you fair, my love, and where do you walk?
Is it near or far away?

Come, my love, while my heart is in the south,
While youth is about my ways—
I will run to meet you and kiss your mouth,
And bless you for all my days.

A MAY SONG.

MAY, May, white May
  Through the village spread ;
Come and make a garland
  Of white May and red.

May, May, sweet May,
  All about the green,
All about the maypole,
  All about the queen.

May, May, red May
  All the lads do wear ;
With whitest of the white May,
  Lasses trim their hair.

May, May, musk May
  Growing in the lane ;
What is half as sweet as May
  Washed with morning rain ?

Red May and white May
  Through the village spread ;
Come and make a garland
  Of white May and red.

DUSK.

THE misty moth-time is begun ;
 Trees stand like shadows in the lanes,
Birds sing their farewells to the sun,
 And candles shine through cottage panes :
And now the west glow softly wanes,
 And crickets about houses run ;
The sky is losing all its stains—
 The night comes on, and day is done.

Repose will ease the workman's pains,
 And speak to him of sleep well won :
He walks in peace along the lanes,
 That have new scent now rain is done ;
Stars come to full light one by one,
 Between wet leaves along the lanes ;
He sees them as he walks, but none
 Cheer him like light through cottage panes.

I LOVE YOU BEST.

YOUR face, the fairest I have seen,
 Is now a part of life to me :
It smiles down sorrows that have been,
 And speaks of pleasures that may be ;
But though you have my heart in thrall,
 I cannot meet you like the rest,
And yet I know, above them all,
                    I love you best.

Your life, the truest I have known,
 Not very sad nor very gay,
Has given guidance to my own,
 That might apart have gone astray ;
So much of good has come to me
 From you that I would now be blest—
Am I unworthy ? Am I free
                    To love you best ?

I cannot flatter in your sight,
 Nor boldly speak as others do ;
But I could suffer, or could fight,
 Or forfeit life for love of you :

Or I could toil for all my days
   To shield you from the world's unrest,
And prove to you, in simple ways,
             I love you best.

Now hopes and fears within me fight,
   As I await the deepest woe,
Or else the richest of delight
   That any youth or man may know;
Soon happiness my heart must fill,
   Or I must turn from peace and rest,
To live a life alone, and still
             To love you best.

BLOSSOMING.

When early blossoms dot the dell
  With gold and white of crimson lip,
And hedges, bright with many a bell,
  Green tassels in the water dip,
Young love is strong, and who can tell
The joy of lovers loving well ?

When Spring drops jewels in the lake,
  And sticks around it stem and stalk,
And kingcups glimmer in the brake,
  And blackbirds to each other talk ;
True pleasure is a lover's meed,
And love in truth is love indeed.

The fairest day-shine is begun,
  The coloured tide of song and scent,
The joyous coming of the sun,
  The time of forest merriment,
When laughter of the birds and trees
Will set a lover's heart at ease.

In the lane the cowslip swells,
   Boughs are amorous of the streams,
Under branching lilac bells
   Lovers dream the old, old dreams ;
Fairies move the leaves above,
Life were nothing without love.

DO NOT FORGET.

'Tis strange to think you go in one short day,
  And that I may not know you any more ;
Why should I fear to look at you and say
  My life can not be as it was before ?
When you return to dear friends you have met
  About your city home where you must dwell,
                              Do not forget
  That some dull village people love you well.

We all have been the better for your face
  And for your merry heart. What shall we do
To raise a smile when you have left the place ?
  My mother will be sad and father too.
When you have gone away to be the pet
  Of " home sweet home " again, I wonder
    whether
                              You will forget
That we have sometimes walked and talked to-
  gether ?

This is the second Sabbath and the last
    That I may sit by you and say these things,
And then some clouds will come to overcast
    My happy sky with dark unfriendly wings;
But there will be a comfort with me yet
    If I may know that you, in busy ways,
                    Will not forget
A cousin and a week of sunny days.

The village folk are coming, one by one,
    Across the fields from church; a little while,
And then this Summer Sunday will be done,
    And I shall grow down-hearted at your smile:
If you should ever think of my regret,
    And what my life out here alone must be,
                    Do not forget
The two names cut upon the apple tree.

D

SPRING.

TIS Spring ! New leaves have come and fields are
　　bright ;
Birds chirrup on the roof at blush of dawn ;
Young butterflies and bees have taken flight,
　　And crocus buds are peeping through the lawn.

'Tis Spring! The leaves are green, and rabbits run
　　In pastures full of daisies, gold and white ;
Brooks shine like silken ribbands in the sun,
　　And babble through the woodlands with delight.

'Tis Spring ! The school-boy by the river side
　　Holds out his fishing rod with anxious look ;
He sees the minnows 'mongst the cresses glide,
　　And fears to breathe when they come nigh his
　　hook.

'Tis Spring ! The linnet trills and cuckoos whoot.
　　From secret woody nooks at close of day ;
When work is done the milk-boy blows his flute
　　Under the hedge, where merry children play.
'Tis Spring ! 'Tis Spring ! O all ye birds that sing
Give out your sweetest strains in praise of Spring !

ABOVE DOUGLAS BAY.

A STRIP of primeval land in the seas,
  Where Progress has rested, but little done
Since the monkish days of the dead Culdees
  (Though the iron horse is learning to run) ;
An island apart from the fretful throng—
  From the sound of trade and the hiss of steam,
Where the jaded may hear a healthy song,
  And dream in a place that is fit for a dream.

There is Douglas town ; it is white with sun ;
  And below,where the lights and shades are blent,
The waves go a-wooing the rocks, and run
  In tides of colour, of song, and of scent.
A world to live in !   There are fields and floods,
  With the song of birds and the sun of seas,
And hills majestic that stretch to the woods,
  Where the oxlips blow, and swing the brown bees.

A canorous wind sweeps up to the hill,
  Like a wingèd organ for ears divine,
With the muffled tones of a cavern rill,
  And breath like a floating draught of wine :

With a kiss that is soft as the touch of silk,
  It comes with a thought that is sweet and cool,
Like the rain after drought, or warm new milk,
  Or the voices of children singing in school.

The ships are rocking themselves to rest ;
  And the bay, with its crescent of shining sand,
Is lit with the waning light of the west,
  Like a piece of sky let down on the land,
Or a charmful glass in a golden frame,
  Where all men may gaze, and some men may
    know
That, while they look up to life without blame,
  They may find the shadow of it below.

The great Sun he gathers his gold, and soon
  His wraith will wander over the waves :
Now, the tide is going to meet the moon,
  And runs from the coves and the weeded caves;
It slips from the sands inwoven with light,
  And the floor of the bay is sleek and bare,
And summer twilight, the daughter of Night
  And of Day, looks into a mirror there.

    *   *   *   *   *

After the noon-blaze, in the breathful eve,
  The many " folk of holiday " come out ;
And lovers saunter on the pier, and leave
  The gossip of their friends, to walk about

The dark'ning shore, where they will nothing say,
  And, though in search of shells, will nothing seek,
And feel that it is pleasant so to stray
  In close companionship, and nothing speak.

Like to a glorious fairy ship afloat,
  With one great sail of light the moon is come;
And people sit in waiting for the boat
  That brings new friends and messages from
    home:

Though there be joys in weeks of quiet life,
  With Mona's many riches to beguile,
The ship that comes from England and its strife,
  Will make the truants in the darkness smile.

IN EDEN.

THE rising sun, with golden touch,
　Brings beauty to the earth and air ;
Ah me ! that there should be so much
　Of sorrow in a world so fair !

The young birds charm the trees with song,
　And praise the sweet year in its youth ;
Ah me ! that we should do the wrong,
　And walk God's garden of the truth !

AN INVITATION.

Dear friend, if you are seeking ease,
Come walk about my forest trees
And meadows green, where rustic ways
Bring tranquil nights and pleasant days—

Where cowslips grow along the brake,
And waxen lilies gem the lake;
Where rabbits through the clover run,
And cresses curtsey to the sun.

I know that you are in the fight
That lasts from morning until night;
I know you struggle hard for wealth,
And take but little heed of health.

'Twill do you good to come and see
The wild blooms blowing on the lea;
To rest awhile where butterflies
Float idly under sunny skies;

A wood where thrushes all the day
Sing songs to boys and girls at play;
Where nightingales below the moon
Pipe many a trembling, throbbing tune.

I promise you the summer scent
Shall fill your heart with merriment;
An idle week in this old wood
Will paint your cheeks and do you good.

TRUE WORDS.

THE words that are true at all times are in winds,
    and in meadows, and seas;
And men that know their own sorrows' and joys,
    may find what they need in these;
They have sympathy subtle with mortals of all
    tongues and of all climes;
They are sad with the sad, and rejoice with the
    glad in happiest times;
They are great with grief as a dirge, or as joyous
    as amorous rhymes.

In Summer to lovers, silent for love, they say the
    things that are best;
They guide to the strongest and richest life, or
    hush to the softest rest;
And when the lovers have older grown, and with
    graver faces they greet,—
These words remind them, above their own, of
    hours and of days that were sweet;
They may not forget the talk of trees and of
    flow'rs that were round their feet.

The child, and the man, and the woman have
feelings they cannot unfold,
But the woods and the brooks tell all to the young
people or to the old ;
By birds and by blossoms are given to the children
wonderful tales ;
And a list'ning, looking man a-field the language
of Nature inhales—
The words of the sun and the moon, and the wind
when it whispers or wails.

The songs that are sung by men unto men are not
to their full desire ;
They say too much or too little ; they lack warmth
or they have too much fire ;
And why should men look for true speech when
they know they cannot comprehend
The words that will tell their own feelings, and
will carry them to a friend
But by the woods and the waters they may find
the true words without end.

EVENING.

Now evening, daughter of the day and night,
  Spreads over meadow-land a dusky shroud ;
The sun, retreating, floods the west with light,
  And hangs a golden lamp on ev'ry cloud.

The fairy butterflies have shut their wings—
  From secret places moths come out to flit,
Or wait in windows till the cricket sings,
  Till doors are closed and cottage candles lit.

Nan, in a pretty cap and simple frock,
  Takes in the snow-white linen from the hedge,
To damp and iron by the kitchen clock,
  And think of Ned who swings the smithy sledge.
The farmer over supper falls asleep
And, snoring, dreams of turnip crops and sheep.

THE PILOT'S GIRL.

ABOVE the cliffs, with her arms on the wall,
　Bare-headed the pilot's bonny girl stands ;
What lad would not climb the rocks at her call ?
　Struggle up to the top to touch her hands ?
But beauty has given no love surmise
　Unto her outlooking over the sea ;
No longing is there in her fine, brave eyes,
　For her whole young heart, as her life, is free ;
Yet a man might feel, should he pass this way,
A strange unrest for a year and a day.

The hedge-born flowers might bring back her face,
　Like to them made fair with a simple life ;
And in notes of the field-birds he might trace
　Faint tones to recall the wondering strife
That beat at his heart when he heard her voice ;
　So might the stray glance of an idle morn
Draw him in uncertain dreams to rejoice
　For a little while, and then feel forlorn ;
And desire would come to soothe his pain
By search for her face and her voice again.

Again by the bay he would long to be,
That once more he might stray where great
cliffs rear ;
He would think of a maiden he might see
In the rose-time of her seventeenth year :
The outgoing gulls again would mingle,
Meeting white home-bending sails from the sea ;
And waves would still shake the sunlit shingle ;
But what to the dreamer would these charms be
If day after day, again and again,
He sought for the face and the voice in vain ?

THE QUESTION.

I LOVE you, Maggie ; you are good—
I have a cottage in a wood,
With melody of boughs above ;
Alas! my cot has not a love.

And throstles drink their morning wine
From dewy cups of eglantine,
And leaves make pleasant noise above—
Come crown my cottage and my love.

I have a little boat to take
My love upon a sheltered lake,
If she will come and faithful prove,
To share my cottage and my love.

The moon looks in the water white,
And nightingales sing of delight
And streams laugh at the stars above—
Come share my cottage and my love.

The early larks to milkmen sing,
And linnets on the lilac swing,
'Mong bells of blue with blue above—
Come share my cottage and my love.

Come to my cot, and you will find
The village people good and kind:
At eve boys play upon the green,
And girls in dainty frocks are seen.

Come to my cot, and you shall see
The ploughman merry as may be,
The blacksmith in his forge as gay
As lovers on a morn of May.

Come to my cot, and I will show
My garden where geraniums grow,
And butterflies and belted bees
Kiss apple-bloom on orchard trees.

Come be my wife, and we will cull
From life the sweet and beautiful,
And earth shall shadow heaven above
If you will share my cot and love.

IN A MEADOW.

How may a grateful mortal speak his thanks
  For such a day as this? The rillet plays
Between a paradise of lilied banks;
  Cool, sheltered by a million moving sprays.
The early sweets of life, that long had been
  Forgotten in the darkened days of pain,
Come back to give old charms to each new scene,
  And withered hopes, like trees, grow green
    again.

Midmost the leafage of the bending lane,
  Half hid in shade, half shining in the sun,
Rumbles the heavy, rocking, farmer's wain;
  And after it barefooted children run
To cheer the waggoner, and reach the hay
  Plucked by the hedges; and old women sit
To knit in silence and to nod away
  The hours on cottage steps with noon-light lit.

THE clouds are pink about day's golden king :
Cool morning gilds the east, and in the west
Black ghosts crawl under earth.   The dingles
    ring
With new-awaken'd life.   Grass blades are drest
In diamond drops.   The bees have taken wing.
The lark has risen from his earthly nest.
The farmer has thrown off his slumbering,
And rosy Jane has had enough of rest,
And comes to milk the cows, and she will sing,
And, smiling, think of him she loves the best.

The dazzling morn has brought a warm delight :
New-budded flowers deck the forest way.
The school-boy in the meadow flies his kite,
And clouds are streak'd with many a sunny ray,
And shining blue behind the shining white
Entices weary travellers to stay,
And sit upon the bank with daisies bright,
While fishes in the tepid river play,
And floating bubbles, fine in colour'd light,
Mirror in miniature the god of Day.

E

The peaceful evening falls : the blazing sun
Paints glory upon earth, and floods the sky
With beauty.   Now the garish day is done
Moths in the dark'ning have come out to fly.
Lights glimmer here and there.   Bats have begun
To flit, and o'er the hills comes melody
Of curfew bells.   The chirping crickets run
On cottage hearths, and dreamily on high
Stars gather round the moonboat one by one,
And night winds sing an easeful lullaby.

SUNDAY MORNING.

The sun, that softer seems on Sabbath days,
  Is showing shadow-trees along the lanes,
And streaming into church by window ways,
    And throwing coloured light from pictured
    panes
Upon the aisle, like Psalms that have no tone :
    One sunbeam through the roof has found its
    way,
And shines athwart the row of saints in stone,
  And worlds of dust are floating in the ray.

The sun is on the preacher's silv'ry head,
  And gives a comfort to his homely words ;
It lights the dim memorials of the dead ;
  'Tis in the ivy, too, with twitt'ring birds :
The listless schoolboys, with their sunburnt looks,
  Glance round to see the sparrow at the door ;
The elder people keep them to their books,
  And poor old folk stare steadfast at the floor.

The organ's prelude to the anthem fills
  The shaded church, and stirs the hearts of men,
Until it sinks to whispering, and stills
  The trembling walls to silentness again;
And now a gentle voice is heard alone,
  Pleading in saintly strains to ev'ry ear,
And winning ev'ry heart with its rich tone—
  A boy's pure treble solo, sweet and clear.

The pray'rs are ended, and all homeward go,
  In twos and threes, by many a pleasant way,
Through woodlands where familiar flowers grow,
  And fields that in their summer growth are gay;
The simple worship of a little while
  Has planted new hopes in the place of cares;
They know the happiness that brings a smile—
  The grace that follows earnest pray'r is theirs.

UNDER A TREE.

THOUGH never so bright
  The sun be at noon,
Yet I have twilight
  And a tinkling tune—
    Under a beech,
    Where the boughs reach
Down to the rill that trickles along,
Playing in beads, and laughing in song;
    And musical sound
    Is wafted around—
Coos the cuckoo, linnets sing too,
In the green tree under the blue.

And soft is the light
  Where peaceful I lie;
And cloud-boats of white
  Sail on in the sky;
    Under my tree
    Sit I, and see
A blending of bloom, a shimmer of streams
Chequered with shadow and shiniest gleams;

And ladybirds come,
And yellow bees hum—
Young pigeons coo, throstles sing too,
In the green tree under the blue.

And as I beguile
The time with a book,
There comes by the stile
A maid with a look
Speaking.of love—
O for her glove !
A word, a smile, or even a pat
Of her hand, or the flower from her hat !
This maid must be mine :
Now let me not pine.
Sing, throstles, sing ; teach me to woo
By the green tree under the blue.

BIRDS IN THE WOOD.

THE birds are in the wood,
Tweet-cheroo, jug, jug-a-jug!
And moss is all ablaze
In the weedy ways,
Cheroo-tweet, jug-a-jug, jug!
The painted butterflies float in the dusky dell,
The brown and yellow bees swing in the woodbine
bell.

The birds are in the wood,
Tweet-cheroo, jug, jug-a-jug;
And my love is in the lane—
In the leafy lane,
Cheroo-tweet, jug-a-jug, jug!
The farmer in the fallow is merry as the morn,
And his waistcoat is red as the poppies in the corn.

The birds are in the wood,
Tweet-cheroo, jug, jug-a-jug;
And I will to my love—
To my loving love,
Cheroo-tweet, jug-a-jug, jug!

And we will laugh and love where rabbits frisk and
    run,
Till the falling of the sun and the day is done.

    The birds are in the wood,
  Tweet-cheroo, jug, jug-a-jug!
   And we'll come home to-night
    In the starry light,
 Cheroo-tweet, jug-a-jug, jug!
Together in the light, tweet-cheroo, jug, jug-a-jug!
Of the starry night, cheroo-tweet, jug-a-jug, jug!

SUMMER EVES.

MY mind is full of memories to-day
  That have the music of old nursery rhymes.
While Kate and Totty here have been at play,
  Have I been in a trance of other times—
Of summer eves that slid by, one by one,
  Like angels passing to another land ;
But they have left their joys, though they are
      gone,
  And lift the curtain with a gentle hand.

It was a summer eve when Arthur came
  And spoke the things that I may not forget ;
The poppies then, as now, were all aflame,
  And there was sweetness with the mignonette.
That night a new moon sailed, and spoke of truth
  That should encircle all our years below :
Our love, like to the moon, was in its youth,
  And there was hope in its faint, tender glow.

A summer eve, again he came to me,
  And I was joyous, who had been forlorn;
We sat together by the apple-tree,
  And ere he left we knew our marriage morn.
That night a half-moon lit the moving length
  Of forest trees; and our love, like the moon,
Had more of gentle light and passion's strength,
  And it would come to sweeter fairness soon.

The summer eves fell into summer days,
  And each bright day new happiness was born,
Till we went by the quiet village ways
  To Abbey Church, and it was marriage morn.
That night the full moon came with glorious shine,
  And showed the garden treasures at our feet;
And our love, like the moon, was full and fine,
  And our divine felicity complete.

SUMMER OF CONTENT.

I REMEMBER a morn behind the mill
    When blackbirds sang,
    And sheepbells rang
Far off, and all things else were still,
    But the rising bream
    In the pictured stream,
And the noise of water about the mill.

I remember a maid in her sweet youth,
    Whose gentle days
    In village ways
Were passed with simple works of truth;
    By her I sat,
    On a moss-made mat,
In a dream of love, in a time of youth.

I remember cuckoo-buds dressed in green,
    The light heart glee
    That came to me,
With the smile of my love at seventeen—
    The laugh that went
    Like woodland scent
To my soul in the sun on the daisied green.

And though I remember the days are spent,
    That love was lost
    When came the frost
At the end of the summer of my content,
    Yet some joy stays
    In winter days,
Because of old kisses and old content.

OLD LOVE AND NEW.

I<small>F</small> Edith use me as a toy
  To kill an idle day,
Or look upon me as a boy,
  To call or send away ;
If she be fickle as the wind,
  Then I'll be fickle too,
And leave her soon, that I may find
  Another maid to woo.

If Fanny care not for a sigh,
  And laugh at all my love,
I will not plead again and cry
  For pity from above ;
If she no longer can be kind,
  Then I'll be kindless too,
And leave her soon, that I may find
  Another maid to woo.

If Katie, who did kiss me once
  In early courtship days,
Should teach me I was but a dunce
  To trust her wanton ways—

If she should learn to change her mind,
  Then I will change mine too,
And leave her soon, that I may find
  Another maid to woo.

If Mary tell me to my face
  She hath no love for me,
Then earth is but a prison place
  Of daily misery.
If she be careless as the wind,
  Still will my soul be true :
I love her so, I may not find
  Another maid to woo.

THE SILENT THRUSH.

POOR thrush! you sit in your wicker cage and
    stare throughout the day;
You know that you are bound with bars, and can-
    not fly away.
And you do not beat the feathers from your wings
    for freedom now,
As you did when you were taken from the swinging
    beechen bough;
Though you can hear your merry mates a-singing
    in the lane,
You sit all day in silence, in the sun or in the
    rain,
And remind me of the ancient king who never
    laughed again.

I wonder, melancholy thrush, if you remember
    aught
Of your partner, and your pleasures in the woods,
    ere you were caught?

Of the dainty fare in fresh fields, of a nest in
    sheltering green—
Do you remember anything of sweet things that
    have been ?
Of mornings in the June-tide when the sun came
    o'er the hill ?
For sure you know all is not well—for sure some
    sorrows fill
That little feathered frame of yours, else why are
    you so still ?

Do you wish that I would go away ? It may be I
    intrude,
But you should not turn your tail to me, for that
    is rather rude ;
Do you think I'm talking nonsense ? that the ill of
    men or birds
Is not to be made lighter by mere sentimental
    words ?
If that is what you mean, my little friend, it may
    be so ;
No doubt you think if I have pity for you in your
    woe
I might help instead of talk—undo the door, and
    let you go ?

And so I will, my lonely friend, for you often make
    me sad
When I sit and see you silent while the other birds
    are glad ;
There ! be at liberty ; the good deed is better than
    the word,
And I feel some blessing on me for helping but a
    bird ;
Ah ! now you are as happy as a little thrush may
    be ;
You look this way as you sing loud upon the apple-
    tree,
And I know that you are singing out your sweetest
    thanks to me.

BIRDS.

O ʏᴇ who complain
Of Life, and are sad,
Come sit in the lane
That summer has clad
In green coats of moss, with flowers begem'd,
Bedotted by buds and with buttercups hem'd,
And listen to birds that flutter and flit,
Trilling, and singing cheroo a-twit-twit,
Twit-twit cheroo, cheroo a-twit-twit.

Fair days quickly run—
Take time as he flies,
And lie in the sun,
'Ere sweet summer dies.
For beauty brings love, and joy in love lies ;
And what sweeter beauty than blue in the skies,
With summer below, and gay birds to flit
'Mong bunches of leaves, a-singing twit-twit,
Twit-twit cheroo, cheroo a-twit-twit ?

Then sit on the grass
With thy love in the lane—
A swain needs a lass,
And a lass needs a swain.
All live things and pretty in forest or field
Woo and are wooed, and unto love yield ;
And the chattering birds that flutter and flit
Have paired and are happy, singing twit-twit,
Piping, and singing cheroo a-twit-twit,
Twit-twit cheroo, cheroo a-twit-twit.

THE SIGNAL.

THE day is come for the ship to sail, and for John
    to go to sea,
And his aged mother is fretting with the bairnie on
    her knee ;
The morning meal is scarcely touched ; and the
    wife is still for sorrow,
For her good man will soon be gone, and she will
    be lone to-morrow :
Black clouds are lowering in the sky, but between
    them streams the sun,
With the light of hope in the dark time that for
    her is just begun.
Oh, may his heart keep as true as hers, and the
    ship in safety run !

And now they are waiting on the beach, and John,
    with uneasy breath,
Is fearing to say the sad farewell—farewell, the
    shadow of death ;

They have little to say, and little know of writing
    in the books,
But though they have lack of words, they can talk
    to each other with looks ;
They can feel the heart in the hand, and read what
    is written in eyes ;
They can tell of their joys and their sorrows in
    kisses and in sighs,
And so can they speak to each other without the
    words of the wise.

There is the good ship, the *Mary Ann*, at her
    moorings in the bay ;
And a boat is grating on the sand, and ready to
    put away
To the waiting ship with John and his mates. Ah,
    there's the signal gun !
And the husband turns to kiss his wife, and they
    to each other run :
It is over at last, and her good man is with the
    other tars ;
She will, weeping, watch the good ship go till the
    dark clouds hide the spars ;
And then for long, lonely nights by the sea below
    the silent stars.

MARY.

MARY can sing—
Not larks that float above the yellow wheat
Can give a touch of melody as sweet
        As she can sing ;
Not brooks that whisper round a wood at night
Can give me half the passionate delight
        As when my love doth sing.

Mary has eyes—
Not blue skies mirrored in a mountain lake
Can from me half such sighing homage take
        As Mary's eyes ;
Not ocean's secret cavern-pools, that glow
In fairy palaces, such beauty know
        As my love's bright brown eyes.

Mary has hair—
You may not such surpassing fairness find
In golden grain, that whispers to the wind,
        As in her hair ;
Not moonlight sleeping on an angel's wings
Is half as sweet, nor aught that nature brings,
        As my love's light brown hair.

Such is my love—
The larks that over yellow wheat-fields float
May to another sing as sweet a note
　　　As does my love ;
But if another would her beauty know,
Let him unto his own fair mistress go—
　　　Fairer is my dear love.

A REST BY THE WAY.

HERE in the sheltered wayside will I stay,
  To look upon this fair place ere I go ;
And sweeten rest where winds harmonious stray
  With just enough of strength to whisper low—
To sway the feathered thistle balls that pass,
And lift faint odours from the meadow grass.

Upon the brook clouds come and drift away,
  And in reflected blue a hammer swings ;
He flinks his tail to show his gold and gray,
  And at his image in the water sings :
A coloured flash ! a moment gone, then he
  Is glinting far-off in another tree.

All things around recall the purer days
  That we have gathered from the troubled years ;
Unto our lips come lines of old-world lays,
  That oft have smoothed our fortunes and our
    fears :
Quaint, simple songs by poets put together,
Under the forest trees in sunny weather.

How happy are they who, in full content,
    Can pass an evening at a cottage door,
Near garden herbs and trees with apples bent,
    And streaming sun upon the sanded floor ;
Who do not wish the light of day to pass
That they may seek the city and its gas.

A DREAM OF A DREAM.

O FOR a bed of buttercups, to rest
  Therein, and watch the summer swallows pass ;
And see the meadow-flowers I love the best
  Among the fairy forests of the grass ;
        That I might seem,
        Without regret,
        In a fair dream
        Of Margaret :
To hold her white warm hand and read her smile,
And feel her kiss again beside the stile !

O for one hour underneath a hedge,
  With boughs of full-blown may-bloom overhead,
Clear water blowing bubbles in the sedge,
  And waving weeds above its pebble bed
        To sink down deep,
        With sun above,
        And have, in sleep,
        This dream of love—
Of love that was, and may not be again ;
Of dear heart-love before it grew to pain !

If the delusion old delight could bring,
   And let me hear the gentle maiden voice
Speak what was spoken once to me, and sing
   The song that made my soul wake to rejoice,—
        Though after sleep
        Came aching truth,
        To bid me weep
        In bitter ruth,—
Yet would I walk again my shadow'd way
Ten years, to dream the dream another day.

TOTTER BELLS.*

How green and long the grass is where we lie,
    In secret, shaded ground !
The laughing wind creeps in, then hurries by,
And the wide fern bends low, and rising, swells,
To set a-swinging all the totter bells,
    That ring without a sound.

How strange that memory should hang about
    A frond of trembling grass !
I see old totter bells, and hear the shout
Of schoolboys running home along the lanes,
Where the sun, swelt'ring in a sea of stains,
    Gilds every pane of glass.

When I was petted in a pinafore,
    And kept a wooden cow,
You stood each side the clock behind the door
Like ears, and when the bells began to sound,
You shook for fear, and fell into a swound
    At that strange, stinging row.

---

* Trembling grass.

And even now are you awaiting woe,
    Though green below the blue ;
And you are sad because the breeze will blow—
Because the giant butterflies will come,
And set the blust'ring bees to swarm and hum
    All day, and frighten you.

BETROTHAL.

I CANNOT tell you of my joy that morn,
When we together walked between the corn,
  And sunniest beams
Were chasing, with soft silver-sandalled feet,
The gliding shadows on the golden wheat ;
  Fair day of dreams !—
Pure dreams prophetical, that all came true,
And gave me love in life and life in you.

That memorable morn began the charm :
The gossips had our story at the farm
  Ere they were told ;
The pigeons seemed to know we should be wed,
And cooed a sweet approval on the shed ;
  And Isaac, old
And white with peaceful years, took me aside
To ask if I had won you as my bride.

I read a fairy book that afternoon,
And through the window came the breath of June,
        To kiss your face,
And honeysuckle nesting in your hair ;
Your father was asleep in his big chair
        By the door place :
Dear time of summer dusk and blossom scent,
Of garden walks in glad bewilderment.

I cannot tell you of my joy that night,
But I remember that the stars were bright,
        And lilacs swung
To cooling wind with gentle rise and fall,
In moonlit clusters by the orchard wall,
        Where roses hung ;
And I remember with new lease of life
I had a precious gift and called it—wife !

IN THE COOL OF THE DAY.

BRING a cushion, my love, and come with me
  For an idle hour in the gath'ring shade ;
We will sit awhile together, and see
  The glow of this summer-lit garden fade ;
Till lights come out at the farms on the lea,
  And the mist veils over the ships at sea.

As we rest in this leaf-lined, bloom-roofed walk,
  We are far from the eyes and ears of men ;
It is as secret for us and our talk
  As a pathless nook in a forest-glen :
Let us stay till the moon looks o'er the wall,
And silvers our haunt like a fairy hall.

The darkness is falling ; the leaves are bent
  With the chilly dew, and the clear drops stand,
Like sensitive charms from elfin-land sent,
  To console the blossoms and bless the land,
And over the roses their guard to keep,
In the moonlit hours of silence and sleep.

While the stars come out, and the glow-worm
    brings
    His lantern to light in the cool hedgerow,
And the nightingale in the forest sings
    Tio-tio, jug-jug, swoot, tio-to;
Let us go indoors, and with pleasant songs,
Remember our joys and forget our wrongs.

MARRIAGE MORN.

This is the sunny marriage morn
Of Clara Winwood, who was born
      In yonder cot
That seems to float upon the corn—
Bright summer and her marriage morn ;
      Would it were not !
The bridegroom walks with happy stride,
But he has only won her pride.

She tames her love and gives her hand
Because he is a lord of land,
      And he can ride
For miles and say, " All this is mine ;
And what is mine, my love, is thine."
      And she can hide
Her soul, and, though her heart be cold,
Put on a smile to get his gold.

There is a youth in Brinton Dell,
And Clara Winwood loves him well :

And he loves her
Unto the very core of truth—
With all the passion of his youth :
                And would it were
That he could prove true love and health
Are far beyond the price of wealth !

Old women tread the churchyard grass
To see the bride and bridegroom pass ;
                And children play
Round gravestones where their sisters sleep ;
And older children know and weep,
                And turn away.
The gossips stand beneath the trees,
And watch and wait in twos and threes.

The belfry shakes, the warm air swells
With merry peal of bridal bells.
                Alas, alas !
For Time will teach the bride by stealth
That love is richer far than wealth.
                Alas, alas !
The bridegroom who can buy and sell
Shall meet the youth of Brinton Dell !

WHILE THE SUN GOES DOWN.

BE with me, pleasant thought, that I may glean
    Fair fancies as I sit here in the shade ;
Be strong for me, my mem'ry, that the scene
    May not be soiled with meaner things, and fade ;
I can recall the pleasures I have known
    In pathless places, in old hopeful days ;
The charm of woodland music idly blown
    About broad boughs in unfrequented ways ;
Now may I print this picture on my brain,
That I may see it in the winter rain.

The hills stretch out for miles, like to a sea
    Stilled into stone in some forgotten age,
And robed with richest growth of herb and tree,
    By passing seasons in their pilgrimage ;
For years in thousands have they stood out there,
    And stared defiance at the tempest's frown ;
And yet to-day they show young colours, fair
    In many mixing tints of green and brown ;
But I forget the frail friends at my feet ;
How very short their lives—how very sweet !

The modest, fair forget-me-not is here :
Who shall forget you ?   Not the lover—no ;
For he would give the bank of wild blooms near
Rather than find you and without you go ;
And still these little gems of tender blue,
That silently confess for timid swains,
Might, simple homely daisies, envy you,
When children find you in the grassy lanes,
And take you with unsullied hands and soft,
And always love you, though they see you oft.

Above the trees, beyond the houseless moor,
The coloured clouds, banked up, conspire to show
Strange palaces with many a golden door,
Where silver floods in jewell'd valleys flow ;
They fade, like fairy cities in a dream ;
The late lights linger of the weary sun,
And now they slowly sink into the stream,
And the cool hush of evening is begun :
Now looming fires appear through cottage panes,
To cheer the homeward walk along the lanes.

AFTERMATH.

Come whisper in this oak, west wind, and blow
A breathing music in among the leaves
To soothe siesta, while haymakers throw
The dying grass that fairy perfume weaves;
And as the pail
Of frothing ale
Is eagerly caressed by sunburnt arms,
I'll dream of country life and rustic charms.

Come, carol in this oak, clear-throated birds,
And let your summer's love be in the lay;
Unto the droning tune of leaves give words,
And in kind fellowship together play;
And I will hearken
Till shadows darken—
Till all the men go home, and cloudlets swim
In glowing amber at the western rim.

JILTED.

THEN tell her this—that now
I have not any wish again to see
A face that has no longer charms for me ;
    And that my vow
Is broken by her own that was not made
With any truth ; that she has only played
False with a man who would have her betrayed.

    My friend, I know her well :
She picked me up that she might put me down
When she had shown a victim to the town :
    But, pray you tell
This young-man-hunter that her loveliest look
Is harmless here ; and that although I took
Her well-trimmed bait, I did not bite the hook.

    There is no love lost, no—
She beckoned me that she might draw the eyes
Of other men to her, and win a prize ;
    And, for a show,

I followed, using her as she used me,
Till I was surfeited; and so, you see,
Her message from a nightmare sets me free.

    Tell her I was unwell
Until her welcome letter came to me,
And filled me full of laughing health and glee;
    And also tell
This flirt—O pity me!—and do not go
To speak these lies; I am too weak to know
My heart in this hour of my overthrow.

THE LAST DAYS OF SUMMER.

No longer, Summer, need you now complain,
   And wish to leave us with your weary band :
Your sister Autumn and her motley train,
   In solemn pomp, are coming to this land.
Much as I love your ways, your scent and song,
   Your sylvan halls of green, your tent of blue,
And all the joys that to your reign belong,
   Yet I must own I love your sister too.

See, even now her messengers appear—
   The woodcock and the snipe from over seas ;
They are not yours, and yet they do not fear
   To fold their wings and rest upon your trees ;
Nor will you fear to seek a sunny isle,
   And gladden it with many a woodland strain
You only leave us for a little while,
   And we shall often wish for you again.

How happy are the swallows to be free,
   That they may find new-budded banks for you !
How eagerly they sail above the sea,
   To spread their wings in skies of warmer blue !

Your true attendants leave you one by one,
'Tis your command, and it is their desire ;
And in a little while you will be gone,
And we shall think of evenings by the fire.

We shall remember you when Autumn makes
The mists to hang for days upon the lea ;
We shall remember you when Winter shakes
The ships a thousand miles away at sea ;
Still, Autumn she will give us fruitful store,
And feasts and festivals will Winter bring ;
But we shall not forget you ; no, before
Dies Winter, we shall sigh to hear you sing.

WATCHING FOR SAILS.

THE morning moaned with sweeping rain;
The wind shrieked with the raging main,
He took the seagulls in his hand,
And, laughing, blew them back to land.

The gulls went out again in glee,
To be carried across the sea;
The wind he puffed them from his hand,
Like bits of paper back to land.

The fishermen went out at night;
The herring-smacks are not in sight—
The wives are paled with tempest wails,
And watch with full eyes for the sails.

The big waves run against the rocks
As they would wake them with their shocks;
And still the wives stand in the rain,
And look for sails at early wane.

The rain it rained and the wind it blew
All day until the darkness grew;

Storm voices then together screamed,
And still wives watched as though they dreamed.

The herring-smacks are in from sea !
The fishermen are home at tea ;
The bairns their little prayers have said,
And go in clean white gowns to bed.

A QUIET NIGHT.

So still the starry night, I almost fear
　My mortal tread, least I should put to flight
A fairy that, for some time of the year,
　Holds court in this old garden by the night.
The flow'rs are broad awake : for very truth
　On this forsaken ground, enchantment dwells,
Such as may breathless hold an am'rous youth,
　Who seeks at dead of night for lover spells,
　With anxious, fearful heart, in haunted dells.

I will not walk, but sit upon this seat,
　That I may see, and hear, and no noise make ;
In time gone by how many gentle feet
　Strayed hitherward to rest for dear Love's sake?
Brave, bright-eyed youths, and many a gentle maid
　Came, haply, here in June or autumn cold,
Leaving the great hall by the portal's shade
　To tell a tale that even then was old—
　How oft at this seat has the tale been told ?

The growing things, it seems, have eyes to see;
  They softly shake their heads, but make no
    moan;
It may be they are whispering of me,
  And wond'ring why I wandered here alone.
I am not waiting for a partner; no,
  You need not point at me for that; the hall
Is rank with ruin; lovers do not go
  To feast together at the baron's call,
  For years they have been dead and buried, all.

How silent! how bewilderingly calm!
  How strange to be in such a place alone!
The big owl on the bough is fixed by charm;
  The cat sits on the wall still as a stone:
Listen! the nightingale! Oh, what a thrill
  Of glory falls on all fair things around!
Now know I why this place has been so still;
  The fairies have shut out all grosser sound
  To hear your song in this old garden-ground.

A SEASON-RING.

AUTUMN.

BEHOLD the full-eared corn! the clustered vine!
The harvest gift to man of wheat and wine:
For these have good folk toiled the long year
    through;
Their daily bread—and cup of comfort too.

WINTER.

The strange sun, like a red moon o'er the land,
Gives sad light to the trees that silent stand,
With all their leafage lost and buried low,
Beneath the white pall of the frozen snow.

SPRING.

New leaves and cowslips deck the frock of Spring,
And in the length'ning evenings new birds sing;
The primrose lifts its young face to the rain,
And bunching hawthorn sweetens heart and brain.

SUMMER.

Now is the beauty of the year broad blown,
With coloured flowers and fronded ferns full
grown—
A paradise for painted butterflies,
That float between green meadows and blue skies.

WAITING.

I KNOW that summer sweets are now broad blown,
That lanes are lined with hedges that have grown
    Green in blue days;
I know that mary-buds have come and gone;
But sunny weeks are dying one by one,
    And my love stays
Behind, so that my winter cares remain:
When joys cannot be plucked they give but pain.

What are the fullest fruits, however sweet,
To one who has not any wish to eat?
    If I could go
With my true plighted love and heart's content
By the Lethean tide of garden scent
    Where blossoms blow,
I would not teach my lips to make complaint,
Nor envy any man, nor any saint.

My love is waiting till the time may be
For her to wed; but Time moves not for me;

The later year
May rob me of the prize that should be mine,
And Time say to another, " She is thine ;"
And so I fear—
While she is growing to full bloom for me,
My soul is starving for what may not be.

All clad in colours will the woodlands be,
In two more months, when Fate will turn to me,
And take or give ;
O may the summer days run quickly by,
And my doubts fall with autumn leaves and die ;
And may we live
To gather love with fruit—our love will be
As rich and ripe as fruit of any tree.

AUTUMN VOICES.

SPIRIT of mournfulness ! chill Autumn wind !
  Making the bare trees shiver as you blow ;
I think I hear you say unto mankind,
  " The flowers are dead, and ye must die also."

Branches that held bloom-tassels in June's day,
  Wither above the water's sullen flow
That sings to men of graves : "Alack-a-day !
  The flowers are dead, and ye must die also."

Man hears, and does not hum the merry ditty
  That spoke his heart when hedges were aglow
With hawthorn, for the leaves say : " Pity ! pity !
  We die ! we die ! and ye must die also."

O wail of water ! heavy lay of leaves !
  You shall not sicken me ; the flowers go
To Paradise, where nothing dies or grieves,
  Ay, there they live again—and man also.

IN THE BAY.

LET me rest on my oars, and breath awhile, before
    I make my way
To the Drake Rock, where the waves are white in
    the middle of the bay:
'Tis too chill these autumn mornings to lie for an
    hour in the boat,
And watch the clouds or the moving craft, or to sit
    with line and float ;
The breeze it is keen ; go in, my oars ; and away,
    my *Good Intent !*
Let us go with a will, and show our love for this
    wild merriment,
Like gulls with the wind in their wings, and the
    brine of the sea for scent.

It was bravely done, my little boat ; and now we
    have made the rock,
That smiles in its grey granite strength at the
    giant sea's roughest shock :

What a feeling of life and of freedom in this
    primeval place !
Where the wind from a wilderness of waves brings
    blood into the face'!
See how each billow rears in its pride as it runs to
    us and swells,
Then breaks on the pebbles with music soft as
    brooks in wooded dells—
No wonder there should be voices in the beautiful
    whiteworn shells.

It is darkening now ; we must put back, for I can
    feel and hear
A coming, whistling, madcap storm that might
    give an old salt some fear.
Right and ready ! ah, now we are running before
    its outstretched hand ;
Warm well to the work, and half-an-hour will
    bring us well to the land ;
We do not make much headway, my *Good Intent*,
    though we seem to glide ;
I remember, tide is against us ; still we are against
    the tide ;
Come, let us strain to our utmost strength ; ah,
    now we ride, we ride !

We are in smoother waters—steady; we have
    beaten wind and tide;
The flying clouds are throwing shadows on the
    barren, bleak hill-side,
And the sun comes out to silver again the sea-gulls
    on the wing;
I know we are nearing home at last; I can hear
    the buoy-bell ring:
Here are the shivering trees once more; they have
    lost half of their gold
Since I went out; the rough wind has laid their
    coloured leaves in the cold:
The days are becoming darker now, for the year is
    growing old.

AT THE FIFTH ACT.

A PLAY, whereof the scenes are bitter-sweet,
  Is acted in young days of ardent truth
By modest maidens fair from face to feet,
  And by their worshippers, aspiring youth.
The first act is as welcome as the sight
  Of a new moon looking through a wood in
    spring ;
The second act and third are full of light,
  And summer warmth and scent of blossoming ;
The fourth act is the eve of harvest-day,
  'When love, large-hearted, beats to melody ;
And then the doubtful fifth act ends the play,
  And makes it comedy or tragedy.

ACT I.

Our life is a wood of fairy fame,
  Where you may enter and behold the spring,
And farther on see summer bloom aflame,
  And hear the birds that through the long days
    sing.

Anon you come to where the late lights blend,
  And find the colour'd autumn trees aglow.
Such is the fairy wood; and at the end
  Are brumal boughs and banks all white with
  snow.
Amelia Wetherland, with eyes of truth,
  Began the strange walk through the changing
  wood,
And at the entrance met a merry youth,
  With sweet surprise of early womanhood.

ACT II.

On Edward Thorpe love like a kind dream fell;
  A moment in a sudden maze he stood,
While passion's piping prelude woo'd him well,
  And with fine glamourie becharm'd the wood;
He lost the fair sight, but the precious strain
  Of silent music slid into his heart,
To be remember'd aye, and to remain
  His winter sunshine or his summer smart.
But there were many pathways, and again
  They met, and were not mute; nor did he miss
The sweetest sweet that he might wish to gain—
  Love quite at love with love, and kiss with kiss.

ACT III.

Amelia met another youth, with eyes
    Of graver greeting, and of softer speech ;
And he had subtle songs of mysteries,
    And wisdom truths romantic he could teach.
His name was Gilbert Gray, and never wight
    Was bound in love with stronger sweeter band.
He saw her eyes, and, dreaming in the light,
    He knew he loved Amelia Wetherland.
Nor had she for his love antipathy,
    But a new passion that had quickly grown ;
So that she gave him her full sympathy,
    And his red bud of promise was broad blown.

ACT IV.

But Edward came again, and simple love
    Grew dearer than the days of deeper truth ;
And Gilbert, who had sat with stars above,
    Was quite forsaken for another youth.
To-morrow morning, and the bridal band
    Will be glad-hearted for the marriage-day
Of Edward and Amelia Wetherland,
    And all will think of happiness who may ;
Love that is lost may turn a darker way,
    And Gilbert he is sunk in malady.
So ends the fourth act ; morrow ends the play—
    Will it be comedy or tragedy ?

BY THE ORCHARD WALL.

When red autumn let the ripe apple fall,
And the tall grass caught it and laid it to rest
With a cool sweet kiss, in a green-covered nest,
The summer dreams sat by the orchard wall.

Side by side we sat with the dreams,
And the singing boughs in a trance
Sang the song of enchanted streams,
And the leaves danced a fairy dance.
The sun-eyed dreams were pure to meet,
Their foreheads were fair as milk ;
Their hair reached down to their feet,
Like buttercups spun to silk :
And the dreams had glorious eyes,
And kisses that charmed to a swoon :
They had stories of Paradise
That were as a heavenly boon ;
For they told not their tale in words,
But spoke to the soul in strains
Of music made by the birds
In unfrequented lanes.

When ripeness let the red apple fall,
  And the cool grass caught it and laid it to rest,
  With a gentle caress, in a shaded nest,
We sat with the dreams by the orchard wall.

AN OLD PICTURE.

THE picture shows her hand upon a skull,
And in between her fingers beautiful
Are some old graveyard thoughts put into rhyme,
And set down in small letters of old time :
> *" Nothing can save*
> *Men from the grave ;*
> *Nothing can heal*
> *A fear we feel—*
> *Ever to seem*
> *Dead in a dream."*

So run the first lines, with their charnel strife,
Between two fingers fine, and full with life.

It was a custom, and an aid to grace,
To paint Death's head below a living face.
What thought the artist ? " Maiden, learn the
    truth ;
Take love, for this it is that follows youth : "
> *" Under the soil,*
> *Curled in a coil*

Of prison clay—
Shut from the day,
And laid down deep
In a death sleep."
But thoughts of death are not in her young mind,
For she is smiling, and her eyes are kind.

Why should a girl, with eyes of gentle fire,
Send her sweet thoughts into the churchyard mire?
Did she live to be three score years and ten,
And did she ever think about death then ?
 " All who have breath
 Must come to death,
 And lie in the dust—
 Unjust and just.
 Nothing can save
 Men from the grave."
The picture hangs above my shelves of books,
With these old verses under lovely looks.

CHANGING PICTURES.

Where are the wild bells that were blue in May,
 The roses that were red and white in June ?
Where are the birds that in the long sweet day
 Charmed the green wood with many a merry
 tune ?
We can but say that now they are not here,
 That happy hours have gone with sunny skies,
That bright-eyed dreams are dying with the year,
 And Summer in her silver coffin lies :
The leaves drop silently about her head—
They cannot live, now that their queen is dead.

Gone is the comfort of the beechen shade,
 The morning scent and the cool sense of ease
That came when showers in the hot days made
 A pleasant music in the full-leaved trees.
We cannot hear the babble of the brook,
 Or see the swallows sailing in the sun ;
We can but on the fading pictures look,
 While the harmonious colours rot and run,
And watch the boughs glow in thin autumn light,
Then turn as black as they before were bright.

And when the canvas is a cheerless thing,
   And droumy days are full of fog again,
And winds that wuther in the wild nights swing
   Upon the reeking poplars in the rain,
We'll tell old stories by the friendly fire,
   And look at pictures painted by the men
Who sat with Summer that she might inspire
   Their brains to take us back to her agen—
Such is their art that we have but to look
To be beside a blossom-covered brook.

And Winter, too, perhaps may make us smile
   With his quaint drawings done in black and
      white,
And then we may forget the flow'rs awhile,
   As we forget the sunshine in the night:
Old Winter likes to tell a ghostly tale,
   And with his pictures we may win delights—
What think you to a good ship in a gale,
   Or frosted fields aglow with cottage lights?
Or skaters blown about in sleety wind,
A red sun sinking in the mist behind?

And then, O happy hope! a little while
   Will free the forest from its winter snow,
And oftentimes a beam of sun will smile
Upon the grass, and warmer winds will blow:

New signs will come upon us day by day,
    And Spring will waken every little tree,
And all our winter thoughts will drop away
    With lilies and new leaves; so will it be
Till Summer comes with many a woodland strain
To sing and paint her pictures o'er again.

RUINED.

HERE is my house; shall I go in
    With ruin round my face?
I worked for many years to win
    This proud and peaceful place;
And now I dare not ring the bell,
    Or move from my own door—
I dare not go, nor stay to tell
    My wife that we are poor.

Now we must leave our wealthy toys,
    And put our pride in pawn;
We cannot play like girls and boys
    At croquet on the lawn;
I may no longer throw the fly
    For trout in my own stream—
O happy home! my wife will cry,
    Because it is a dream.

Love that rejoices in a cot
    Is not the love for me,
I should have what I shall have not
    To be what I would be;

I

Now I must earn a workman's fee,
　And perhaps my wife will stitch—
There is no peace in poverty
　For men who have been rich.

A storm broods, and is coming near,
　It suits my state of mind;
The willows in their hour of fear
　Turn white leaves to the wind.
The clouds, that erewhile hung aloof,
　Meet, and the rain-drops fall;
The tempest is about my roof—
　About my heart, and all.

WAITING FOR ESCORT.

I.

How full of loss is love! A fair girl's face
    For lack of lover's lips may lose its light;
And souls astray, that seek in vain the place
    Where their love lies, may never live aright.
And when two kindred hearts in courtship meet,
    And in the crowd unto each other cling,
He may be slowly drawn to other feet,
    And she may hear a wealthy, wise man sing.
How many, without doubt, go hand in hand
    Across the waves of passion's restless sea,
And find contentment in a quiet land?—
    I dare not think how many such there be.
A maiden by the flutter of her fan
May spoil the strong life of a bearded man.

II.

And yet how full of gain is love! Ah me!
    What other thing could wear us to our woes
When all our ways are strewn with treachery,
    And we have friends who are but smiling foes?

I 2

How could we live by them, and near them sleep,
    And still find happy moments of relief?
How could we from their throats our fingers keep,
    But that the house of love would come to grief?
And when our paths are clear, and fleck'd with
        sun,
    And radiant flow'rs in moss-grown gardens lie,
Where peaceful days harmoniously run,
    Love is the only sweet that will not die:
A faithful maid, and then a loving wife,
May give the poorest man the richest life.

III.

And yet how full of loss!   Eliza Lisle,
    Long have I watched you in your maidenhood;
And I have seen you by a careless smile'
    Bring to the cheek a young man's eager blood.
When Donald came to woo your Spanish face,
    I thought that some day he would come to wed;
I know the night you promised, and the place,
    And you were happy, though you no word said.
When morning woke with sparkle of wet grass,
    And thin light on late summer's fading bloom,
You saw your face all laughter in the glass,
    And sang a ballad ere you left your room—

Then like a beggar he must come, and so
You turned, and, like a beggar, let him go.

IV.

There is deep winter now in Donald's purse,
 And in your thoughts he cannot play a part;
But you have brought on him a greater curse,
 And placed the depth of winter in his heart.
The thing you call your love is made, it seems,
 Of such fine stuff it must have dainty fare;
And now Sir Dummy Dawdle has sweet dreams,
 Because you let him sit in Donald's chair.
He carries keys to open every door
 That leads to gaiety and easy life,
And you may leave behind the staring poor,
 And be a silk and satin, scented wife.
Love you your true love, be he rich or poor,
But do not leave him when he has no more.

V.

This is a night of triumph, 'Liza Lisle;
 In your dark face your eyes like stars are set;
Your pretty mouth has moved with many a smile
 This day—this day that you will not forget.
Now you at last are ready for the ball,
 In swathing clouds, a beautiful brunette;

Why hastens not your lover through the hall
   To look with pride upon his little pet?
He will not please you more with song or jest;
   You will not dance to-night, nor hear the band—
He has a broken dagger in his breast,
   And Donald has the red haft in his hand.
Now, lady, live the next hour as you may—
You laugh, but it is Donald comes this way.

SUMMER'S WRAITH.

THE sun went wanly down last night,
　　And the attendant clouds
Showed no rich colours in his light,
　　But hung about like shrouds ;
Nor were the wide hills robed with wonted gold,
But garmented with gloomy grey, and cold.

Soon, soon the bloom will find its blight ;
　　And soon the leaves will go,
In days that are not dark nor light—
　　That have not sun nor snow ;
With neither frost nor flow'rs to trim the lane ;
But sunless days, and starless nights, and rain.

I turned away with thoughts like these,
　　And went toward the wood ;
And when I reached the moveless trees,
　　A maid before me stood :
Some forest blooms drooped from her girdle down,
With dew-drenched leaves, half yellow and half
　　brown.

She seemed as in a world alone :
 The wreath fell from her head ;
She sighed ; then, going, made a moan ;
 And flow'rs dropped from her dead ;
And nothing more I saw of her, but heard
The sad song of a solitary bird.

Surely it was no mortal thing,
 But summer's wraith, I saw ?
I stood and heard the murmuring,
 Of trees struck with a flaw ;
And then there came a shock that chilled my
  blood,
Of blund'ring winds bewintering the wood.

AUTUMN RAIN.

THE mornings come with a chill,
   And mist by the meadow hedge ;
A cold wind creeps by the mill,
   And tall reeds shrink in the sedge :
The brook has lost the swallow,
   And the bush has lost its may ;
On upland and in hollow
     There is decay.

The sparrows sit on the shed,
   Sit and sit, and no word say ;
And the sun is blurred and red,
   In sky that is gloomy and grey.
Men carry a load of care—
   Children seem sadder at play,
For in the fields that were fair
     There is decay.

The bare black branches shiver,
   And shake dead leaves in the wet :

The rain is on the river,
And fog in the city is set ;
And no birds fly in the air—
No flowers gladden the day,
For all that summer made fair
Is in decay.

The darkness comes, and a line
Of ghost-like lamps in the night,
With yellow dim lights, shine
On faces woefully white ;
No roses to scent the air—
No moonlit green tree way,
For in the world that was fair
There is decay.

WAITING FOR WINTER.

THE autumn colours deepen into gloom:
  The cold winds come, and it is time to light
The first fire of the winter in my room,
    To warm the hearth and make the ceiling
      bright—
  King Coal, I welcome you this dreary night.

Be kind to me, as you have ever been,
  And do not chide because in sunny times
I quite forgot you under hedges green,
  A-listening to the jocund summer chimes,
  In dreams of dear new love and sweet old
    rhymes.

Believe me, my dear friend, a brook in June
  Has given greater joy than well-earned gold ;
And I have been the better for the tune,
  But dearer are the stories you have told
  When frosty wind has whistled on the wold.

Give me a sign ; yea, now I see the flames
  In curling colours glow and rise and blend ;
Upon the embers are familiar names,
  And well-known faces in the smoke ascend ;
  And now I know that you are still my friend.

I sit before you with a pleasant fear
  To see remembered pictures of dead days—
To watch myself walk through the dying year—
  To meet my friends and foes by many ways,
  And do my part in still unfinished plays.

I wait for winter and his wild, white nights,
  And many of them will I spend with you ;
And my dull room shall then have fairy lights,
  Reflected from your flames of red and blue ;
  And many old tales shall be told anew.

NOT FOR LOVE.

HELEN was fair, indeed, and I was free ;
But that which had been was not so to be—
My heart awoke, and Helen guided me ;
        But not for love.
In winter deep I dreamt of summer shine,
And all my hopes were false as they were fine.

And I was happy then as I might be :
Warm spring had painted every field and tree ;
And Helen sang sweet ditties unto me ;
        But not of love.
And I had looked upon her budded youth
As on a book of innocence and truth.

And knowing not of poison in the wine,
I said, " And may I link my life with thine ?"
She whispered, " Yes," and placed her hand in
   mine ;
        But not for love.
And I was in a sweet swoon of delight,
And thought it daytime in the depth of night.

'Twas coming soon, too soon, when I should keep
My days in darkness and my eyes from sleep ;
When Helen, without sorrowing, should weep,
                              And not for love.
O that a maid should sigh upon her glove,
And mimic fondness where there is no love !

BRIDAL BELLS.

WHO shall say
How happy Charlotte is to-day !
She goes to church with blossoms white,
And to-night is her bridal night.
For her the village children go
To line the churchyard path, and throw
Fair forest favours at her feet :
For her, flags flutter in the street ;
There is sunlight under the leaves,
And the bride in her fancy weaves
Long pleasures for after days,
In summer's pleasant ways.
The night of waiting is done,
And love is crowned in the sun :
The glad bells ring, ding, ding-a-dong,
And laugh in the bridal song.

Who shall say
How sad Lucinda is to-day ?
At her window with eye-lids wet,
She remembers what others forget.

Summer may come and south winds blow
Seed from the grass, and bees may go
Home with pilfered honey at eve,
And she forget it all to grieve.
She was won in an idle day,
Worn a little and thrown away;
And he who wooed forgets it now
In church at his marriage vow.
The day of her hope is done,
And her love lies dead in the sun.
The sad bells ring, ding dong, ding dong,
And weep in the wedding song.

WHEN THE WIND BLOWS.

O THE dancing of the leaves,
    When the wind blows !
And the rushing noise of trees,
Shouting, shrieking on the leas,
Like the sound of seething seas,
    When the wind blows !

O the bending of the boughs,
    When the wind blows !
The moan and the quiver
Of reeds along the river—
That sink, and rise, and shiver—
    When the wind blows !

O the shifting of the clouds,
    When the wind blows !
Sailing swiftly on between
The wide blue world and the green,
Throwing shadows o'er the sheen,
    When the wind blows !

K

O the drifting of the snow,
When the wind blows!
Showing in the cold moonlight
Fallen trees hid under white,
Like great ghosts in bed at night,
When the wind blows!

O the comfort of the fire,
When the wind blows!
To hear the song and the chat
Of the kettle and the cat,
And the cricket on the mat,
When the wind blows!

THE BRETBY BELLS.

WHAT a night for a walk by wood and moor!
  I cannot see you though I have your arm,
And we have seven miles to go before
  We reach the gate, and Snarler gives th' alarm!
At home they may be thinking we are lost,
  Without the moon or stars to lend us light;
There's not a thing to see, not even frost;
  At least they'll know that it is Tuesday night.

For more than thirty years our Bretby bells
  Have rung on Tuesday nights in winter-time;
They're rather cracked, but with them music swells
  Sweeter than with a more harmonious chime:
You may trust to the bells on Tuesday night;
  A child may be born or a man may die,
It may rain or snow, or be dark or light,
  But they always ring—I will tell you why.

You may hear them now though they're miles
      away;
  We could make for them in fog or in frost,
And while they are ringing we cannot stray
  Far from our path on the moor, and be lost:

They know this at home when the hearth is
    bright,
And fear will not make them stop in their song :
But why do they ring ev'ry Tuesday night ?
I will tell you why as we walk along.

Many years ago, before I was born,
    Or steam to our village had made approach,
When the Bretby people could hear the horn
    That was blown by the guard of the coming
      coach,
There was an old parson called Peter Moss,
    Who guided his flock in a godly way ;
Every Tuesday he walked to Dulmer Cross,
    Out here by the moor, to preach and pray.

He used to leave Bretby soon after three,
    To make the poor Dulmer people divine ;
For years he was home to his time for tea,
    Which his wife had ready for him at nine.
One December night when the way was black,
    It was thought that the parson was lost on the
      moor ;
It was ten o'clock, and he was not back,
    And at twelve he had not reached his door.

His wife had fallen asleep in her chair ;
  She woke at the striking of twelve o'clock,
And a tempest was in the midnight air,
  And her husband ! she had not heard him knock !
She sat in despair—how the wind did shout !
  What could she do ? Her two sons were abed,
And asleep, and the village lights were out :
  And where was her husband ? Perhaps he was
    dead !

Was he lost on the moors ? Upstairs she went,
  While the wind was rising in moaning swells,
And in her despair her two sons she sent
  With the key of the church to ring the bells.
While they went with a lantern, half asleep,
  She ran to the ringers and waked them all :
Not one of them back to his bed did creep,
  But each man was true to the good wife's call.

And they rang a mad peal with all their might,
  That could have been heard to the end of the
    moors,
And the village folk came out in the night
  To wonder and stare at the cottage doors ;
Some thought the French were invading the land,
  That the men would be called away to fight,
And march from the village behind a band,
  And they shivered and talked in the winter night.

A sound was heard in the early morn
Of a galloping horse in the frosty lane,
And old Peter Moss on the steed was borne,
To his Bretby home and his wife again.
He was lost till he heard the good bells ring;
Then he found a horse, and he knew he was
right;
He could hear the bells nearer and nearer sing;
And that's why they're ringing and singing to-
night.

WINTER WEATHER.

THE bleachèd snow is come, and chill winds blow ;
Under the eaves are icicles a-row ;
And old men wheeze ; the village milk-pails freeze,
And school-boys slide to school along the leas.

Cold stars alight in the clear keen night,
Stare on bleak moors with earnest eyes and bright ;
The fire-flames leap, and thither old wives creep ;
The cat is curled up on the hearth asleep.

A BEGGAR MAN.

WHO is this standing in the street
With white face bending o'er bare feet?
Why does he go about like that—
Without a coat, without a hat?
He looks as though a little food
Would make him smile, and do him good.
And why does he not go away?
He's talking now: what does he say?

———

" Where shall I drag these bones of mine
    That ache because my rags are thin?
O for the food that even swine
    May eat, and straw that they lie in!

" How all the people pass me by
    This Sabbath eve, and see me not;
The many bells how joyously
    They ring that care may be forgot!

" Yet if I were to ask for bread,
   Or shelter from the bitter flaw,
I might be as a vagrant led,
   To hear the mighty Christian law.

" Still let me not blaspheme, O Lord !
   Or speak Thy name with aught but good ;
They do abuse Thy Holy Word
   As they abuse my want of food.

" For truly Thou didst go about
   The Comforter of all poor men ;
Thou wouldst have surely found me out,
   And bade me come to Thee again.

" The Church, how peacefully it stands,
   With painted panes amongst the trees ;
The sinner clasps his jewelled hands,
   And there are cushions for his knees.

" I will not judge, but only crave,
   If thou shouldst give again to me
A loaf to eat, a pound to save,
   That I the beggar man may see.

" Let me remember what I know,
   And it will chain me to his side,
So that the beggar shall not go
   Till we Thy blessings, Lord, divide."

A WINTER NIGHT.

AWAY sleet ghosts in wild wind go !
  And the walls are white
  In the winter night,
And cottage windows, rimm'd with snow,
  Are red with red fire-light.

The moon sails in the stormy main,
  To glide and to glance;
  And the shadows dance,
And fly together down the lane,
  And round the haunted manse.

Here is the hamlet's quiet way;
  And here would I be,
  Where the winds are free—
There is the city far away,
  With lamps like lights at sea.

ABEL KARE.

His head was bald, and white the hair
Upon the chin of Abel Kare;
His legs were shrunken up, and thin,
And his big bones stretched out the skin;
His eyes were dim, deep in the skull;
And his cup of life with years was full.
The room was dark, and Abel Kare
Alone sat in a creaky chair
That mocked the cricket, and often too
Would mock the groan in the chimney flue!
The wind it made the great trees shriek,
And bent their necks, and made them creak,
In ghostly voice (a little mouse
Came out to see what shook the house
And ran in fear), and the rush-made chair
Seemed glad of the howling in the air,
And cried and creaked to Abel Kare.
Abel sat alone in his room,
Watching the flame-light in the gloom—
Watching the fire-balls, seething white,
Turn red in the grate. " I'll have a light;

I've a bottle, a candle too,
And I have gold—ah, ah !"   Whew, whew !
O heaven ! the screaming wind it blew
Down the chimney, round the house,
And to its hole the little mouse
Ran in fear ; and more red and red
Gleamed the embers, and overhead,
Above the housetops, louder blew
The wind, and fierce the tempest grew.
" How it blows ! I'll have a light ;
It is a very furious night ;
Who have not got them gold must fare
As cats and dogs," said Abel Kare.
The candle burnt a deadly flame,
And dark and darker the room became ;
Fiercer and redder the embers grew,
Louder and louder the wind it blew !
And then—another rush-made chair !
And in it another Abel Kare !
Abel of flesh, to Abel of air,
Said, as he shifted back in his chair,
" What are you, and why do you stare ?"
Abel of shade, to Abel of blood,
Said, " I'm yourself, and nothing good.
Abel Kare, there's nought can save
A man from death, and from the grave.

All the world knows you're a miser,
And a scorner, a despiser,
And you shall gather scorn and hate—
You shall carry a golden weight.
Put all your money in a sack,
And carry it upon your back,
And find the man you turned away
In hungry craving yesterday;
And you shall tread the crowded street,
And nothing drink, and nothing eat
Until the beggar-man you meet ;
And if you find him not you die,
And in your grave the gold shall lie,
To shame you in your second day.
Now get your gold, and come away."
Abel of shade and Abel of bone
Went in the snow and the windy moan;
And many years they have been gone.
Abel of blood carried the sack
With all his gold upon his back,
And with his weight he walked before.
Abel of shade a coffin bore ;
A plate was on the lid, and there
Was the name of Abel Kare.

SIGH NOT SO.

Sigh not so for summer weather—
  For the hot sun and the blaze
Of the bloom upon the heather ;
Sigh not so for summer weather,
  And the glory of long days.

Winter holds a friendly hand,
  With a quaint book of romance,
Written in old Wonderland,
While the fairies, hand in hand,
  Joined their laughter with the dance.

There are flow'rs of purest white
  In his book, and you may find
Pictures painted in the night,
When the land with snow was white,
  And the trees were bent with wind.

Many ballads of the brave—
  Many legends of the just—
Many songs for love to save,
Sung in castles of the brave
  That have crumbled into dust.

Sigh not so for summer weather—
For the sun, and greenwood ways :
Let us go along together,
Thankful for the winter weather,
And the promise of new days.

THE COMING SNOW.

THE clouds were copper-dyed all day,
And struggled in each other's way,
Until the darkness drifted down
To the summer-forsaken town.

Said people passing in the lane,
" It will be snow," or " 'Twill be rain ;"
And school-bairns laughing in a row,
Looked through the panes, and wished for snow.

The swollen clouds let nothing fall,
But gath'ring gloom that covered all ;
Then came a wind and shook his wings,
And curled the dead leaves into rings.

He made the shutters move and crack,
And hurtled round the chimney-stack ;
Then he swept on to shake the trees,
Until they moaned like winter seas.

Soon he went whistling o'er the hill,
And all the trees again stood still ;
Then through the dark the snow came down,
And whitened all the sleeping town.

The keen stars looked out through the night,
And flecked the boughs with flakes of light ;
Then moving clouds revealed the moon
That made on earth a fairy noon.

Then Winter went unto his throne,
That with a million diamonds shone ;
A crown of stars was on his head,
And round him his great robes were spread.

At morn the bairns laughed with delight
To see the fields and hedges white,
And folks said as they hurried past,
" Good morning ! winter's come at last."

L

BURNT WINGS.

How deep a life has love! Three years of pain
   Have not aroused me from my overthrow;
Three summers washed with show'rs of scented
     rain—
Three winters whitened with the silent snow,
Have left me comfortless, and like to one
   Who stands half conscious in a crowded street,
And seeking for his mem'ry that is gone,
   Forgets the purpose that should guide his feet.
O where is Pity, that a maid should say
Sweet things unfelt and blight a life in play?

And where is Reason, that a man should cling
   To dead dreams and delusions of his youth;
Is life so small that I may only sing
   One song, and die because of one untruth?
No, I am young in earth's great wilderness
   Of beauties; why then faint upon the brink?
I will go forward for new happiness,
   And in the search forget the broken link.

Forget ?   I do forget myself indeed,
To think that Reason should have pow'r to plead.

On such a quest how find Promethean sparks,
  With passions locked up and the gold key lost ;
I should mistake all weathercocks for larks,
  And meadow mist of Summer morn for frost.
I cannot bid one half my heart be still,
  And if I could, it is not in my power ;
A maid to gratify her own sweet will,
  Asked for my love to wear it as a flower—
O what a hope of joy !   What need to say
I gave it, and she flung the thing away.

POVERTY'S WINTER.

RAIN is making rings on the river,
And dead leaves in the black trees shiver ;
Desolate sparrows under the shed,
Dream of the summer and crumbs of bread.

O the rain in the cold winter time !
And bitter bread that is bought by crime !
The fog and frost from morning till night,
Nor coals to burn nor candles to light.

The time is coming ; summer is dead ;
Winter thickens the clouds overhead ;
And soon the snow will lie at the door,
And the poor will know that they are poor.

JE VOUS ADORE.

I WILL not say you're fairer far
Than angels that in heaven are ;
I will not falsely flatter you,
But I will tell you what is true—
              Je vous adore.
Mon amie chérie, je vous adore.

I knew you for a little while—
I heard your voice, I saw you smile ;
And as you moved among the throng,
I looked, and learnt this two-line song—
              Je vous adore.
Mon amie chérie, je vous adore.

The night died out, the morning came,
The big sun set the sea aflame :
We walked together by the sands
And waves sang as we joined our hands—
              Je vous adore.
Mon amie chérie, je vour adore.

Dim evening faded into night,
The yellow moon turned small and white,
And, floating o'er the trees, the chime
Of curfew bells breathed out the rhyme—
                    Je vous adore.
Mon amie chérie, je vous adore.

When sails the ship that brings me home
To friends, and fields we used to roam,
Will it be well for me to sing
This posy of a lover's ring—
                    Je vous adore.
Mon amie chérie, je vous adore ?

THE FIRST SNOWFALL.

THE leafless trees were black and wet,
   Half hid in chilly mist, last night—
This morn each wears a coronet,
   With purest crystal fires alight.

We in the dark with dreams were still,
   When silently the elves came down,
To throw a great robe round the hill,
   And muffle all the sleeping town.

The sceptre is in Winter's hand—
   His willing troop of Northern fays
Have thrown his jewels o'er the land,
   In their enchanted midnight maze.

The hall seems, as it stands alone
   With red sun on its frosted panes,
Like a palace to dreamers shown
   In a proud fairy lord's domains.

Here is the robin, welcome guest ;
    And he is cheerful in the flaw—
The amulet upon his breast
    Will shield him in the icy shaw.

Bright bird, you bring again the joys
    That made us happy long ago,
When we were little girls and boys—
    When first we saw you in the snow.

How merry will the children be
    When they awake !   It makes me smile
To think how they will shout to see
    White fields and woods for many a mile !

What a sweet wonder is the year,
    With seasons charming all our days !
We wait for Winter with some fear,
    But beauty is in all his ways.

DEAD DAYS.

I CANNOT let lost life with lost years go—
I must look back to what I used to know,
     And looking weep:
I must remember that my double life
Of happiness is now a single strife,
     And that you sleep
All through the longest days of summer glow,
And through the longest nights of winter snow.

Love played with us in youth time, and he came
Along with us in after-days the same,
     With joy and rest;
The pleasant months grew into changing years,
And changing pleasures chided little fears
     From our sweet nest:
I must remember that my whole life grew
In fairer, braver ways, because of you.

I cannot help my heart, my tears must flow,
And though the sun is on me, I must know
A day that died ;
The frightened clock ran down—O, bitter spite !—
From twelve at noon to twelve o'clock at night ;
And fever-eyed,
I live in body, but my heart is dead
Like a dry leaf upon a spider's thread.

Death is the price and penalty of life ;
Our vow was—till he parted us, lost wife ;
Yet thought we not
That one would die, and one find months and years
Blank days made up of neither hopes nor fears.
It is the lot
Of all ; to meet again an old faith too ;
God of us all ! what if it should be true ?

WINTER WALKS.

PLEASANT it is in the morning to see
The snow untrodden ; the frost on the tree ;
To face the bleak wind, and merrily go
On foot to the town in a healthy glow.

Pleasant it is in the night to retreat
From the flaring gas in the noisy street—
To leave the shops, and the crush, and the cars,
For the country, keen skies, and crowds of stars.

MY LADY'S FAVOURS.

You have not seen my Bessie ?—beauty Bess—
　　She is a shrew, a very pretty shrew ;
Cheeks like a blush-rose leaf, sweet eyes and lips,
　　Belong to Bessie, and she knows it, too,
　　　　　　And it has taught her coquetry,
　　　　　　She will not be what I would be—
If I be so, why then so is not she.

If I am shy at Bessie, bonny Bess,
　　She looks and laughs, and is not shy at me ;
But if I show her that I am not shy,
　　She glances down, and very shy is she ;
　　　　　　There's nought, not even flattery,
　　　　　　Will bid her be as I would be—
If I do so, why then so does not she.

If I but smile at Bessie, beauty Bess,
　　Straightway she turns aside and seems amiss ;
But if I seem amiss and go away,
　　She comes with loving looks to beg a kiss ;
　　　　　　Nor coolness nor civility
　　　　　　Will bid her be as I would be—
If I agree, why then so does not she.

If I be dull, my Bessie, beauty Bess,
   Will mock a sigh, and titter and be glad ;
If I be boisterous and very blythe,
   O very still is she and very sad!
            Big boldness nor meek modesty
            Will bid her be as I would be—
If I would so, why then so would not she.

And yet I love my Bessie, birdie Bess !
   And I shall ask a question : if a nay
Be her reply, I'll tell her woman's nay
   Is but a yea, so be it nay or yea,
            'Twill bid her be as I would be.
            So once I think we shall agree,
And when I go to church, why so will she.

ON THE HILL.

HERE is the hamlet on the hill,
  The city is below;
And here men's hearts and homes are still,
  And there they are not so—
The snow is white upon the hill,
  And it is black below.

Here is the hamlet and its rest,
  But little rest below;
And here the life we love the best,
  Where winds untainted blow;
And here the peace and here the rest
  That are unknown below.

ENCHANTED EMBERS.

WHEN bright flames flicker o'er the burning coal,
  And throw gaunt shadows on the dusky walls,
And my black cat sits by the mouse's hole
  With two round glaring eyes like fiery balls,
Then in the ruddy, sympathetic blaze
I see old friends and live in olden days.

Live o'er again a time that was to this
  As sunny summer is to winter's cold:
As restless troubles are compared with bliss,
  Are present days compared with days of old.
What now is out of reach I wish it here,
And that which cannot be is doubly dear.

See, in the dreamy glamour of the grate
  Come the quaint pictures of my boyhood's prime;
I swing again upon the farmer's gate,
  And hear the sheep bells, and the evening chime
Floating o'er gabled roofs with drowsy hum,
And telling of the happy days to come.

Days that have come, alas ! without the joy,
    Without the golden hours, without the wealth,
And all the fame I dreamt of as a boy
    Full of high hope, and bright with rosy health,
I did not think of weary ways beset
With sickness, death, and with continual fret.

I did not think on't then, nor will I now,
    Although 'twill come with sunlight on the
        morrow—
Thy aid, forgetfulness ! O teach me how
    To banish all remorseful thoughts of sorrow ;
O let not penury have power to craze,
And keep calamity from out the blaze.

Ah ! now I see the house where I was born,
    The sleepy village, and the pebbled brook ;
The meadow pathway, daisy-edged and worn,
    The lazy mill and many a woodland nook
Where I have stayed whole hours, 'neath oak trees
        hoary,
Deep in the spell of some fantastic story.

Dim legends that of chivalry do tell,
    Of Arthur bold, and of the Red Cross Knight
Who overcame the power of magic spell,
    And with the fearful Dragon fiend did fight,

For love of that fair lady, Una hight,
And for the love of Errantry's bright light.

Why mingle in imaginary strife ?
 Why dream of poets and of old-world lore ?
Of honeyed peace and simple country life,
 To make the city duller than before ?
No, let us not repine in murky weather,
The sun will shine again and gild the heather.

The mystic flowers of romance have grown
 To mandrakes, and no more are friends of mine ;
The veil is ta'en away, and truth hath thrown,
 The root of hemlock in the fairy wine,
And what was once a solace now destroys,
So the rude Real slays fair Fancy's joys.

Ah ! . . . Hedges are just washed with April
 rain,*
And shimmer softly in the noonday light,
Cold shadows chase each other o'er the plain,
 Coming and gliding by in dreamy flight,

---

* The writer wishes to state that this line was not taken
from Longfellow's " Keramos " :
 " ' Just washed by gentle April rains.' "
"Keramos" was published in 1878. "Enchanted Embers,"
the writer's first published verses, appeared in the *Dark Blue*
magazine about 1870 or 1871. The writer may also state, in
reply to several who have mentioned the matter, that

And trembling leaves, with swelling buds between,
Make up a charm of blushing white and green.

And now 'tis summer, and sweet gossamer
   Is hung from twig to twig for elves to swing
By moonlight when rude feet are not astir,
   When bright Titania bids her birdie sing ;
When Oberon cheers the happy band, and when
Puck tells of all his gambols among men.

I see a cosy room with ivy sprays
   That tap the panes and through the window peep,
And on the hearthrug, where a kitten plays,
   A boy sets up tin soldiers half asleep.
The cricket chirups, and a tall brown clock
Conducts the kettle's song with steady knock.

    *   *   *   *   *   *

E'en now I cannot tell you what I see—
   It is too full of hazy joy to preach ;
If heart-throbs and big tears could speak for me,
   Then I should be more eloquent in speech :
O ! cherished home and friends true to the core,
I never knew how dear ye were before !

he did not take his title " Aftermath " from the same source
the verses with this title having appeared years before in
Cassell's Magazine.

BY THE HEARTH.

THE dark lane is lonely to night :
 How the tempest shrieks !
 And the great oak creaks
And groans in the furious fight.

Let us put down the blind, and turn
 From the window-pane,
 And the wind and rain,
To the tea and the singing urn.

The children, with bright happy looks,
 Have covered the floor
 With a motley store
Of their toys and their fairy-books.

Of the spring and the summer we tire,
 But we may find joy
 To last and not cloy,
At play with the bairns by the fire.

Town gaieties who can **endure** ?
The life that is best
We find when we rest
At home by the hearth—it is pure.

HOW LONG ?

How long shall I wait for my love, how long ?
    When shall I see him and know he is mine ?
In spring I was joyous, for hope was strong,
    But the spring was lost in the summer shine,
    And he came not—O Love ! how long ?

For lazy hours in the flowering June,
    I waited, and wandered to meet my fate,
And I bowed, as lovers will, to the moon,
    For luck in my love, but my truant mate
    Came not, and I had still to wait.

The comfortless autumn came with its gloom,
    And I sat by the fire long, lonely nights,
With the weary clock in my dingy room,
    Still looking for love in the ember lights ;
    Till I began to fear my doom.

Now meadows are muffled with moveless snow,
  And winter again is cruel and strong ;
He has frozen my heart, and now I know
   The truth at last—that to death I belong,
   And not to Love—O Death ! how long ?

A WHITE WOOD.

THE wood is white with feathered fans of snow,
　And with the burden barren boughs are bent;
And when the frosty winter wind doth blow,
　A pearly dust unto the path is sent:
　　　And the stream lies dead
　　　In an icy bed;
But fairies have covered her brow with beads,
And hung crystal crowns on willows and weeds;

　　　And in the spring
　　　Throstles shall sing,
And daisies shall dot the green of the grass,
For girls and for boys to pluck as they pass;
　　　And the stream shall awake
　　　To rejoice in the day,
　　　And with love-laughter shake
　　　All the flowers on its way;
And there shall be clusters of red and white may—
A fair moon by night and a fine sun by day.

But the wide wood is white
In this time of blight,
And the sun is but showing
A shadow of light,
And the darkness is growing
Before it is night.
A sadness doth fill
The dale and the hill—
The robin seems chill
In the tree that is black,
In the wood that is still;
And white in a swoon
Sun sinks, and the moon
Is beginning to float,
Like a pale phantom boat ;
And the cottage smoke curls up in a dream
Of despair and of doom,
And is lost in the gloom
That gathers and reddens the firelight gleam.

Let us leave this white wood, and thoughts that
    are dire,
For the warmth of the hearth and the flame of
    the fire.

THE GARDEN SEAT.

THE garden-seat was overgrown in spring
  With young, sweet flowers swathed in purest
    green;
I saw a little child her toy-book bring,
  With pictures of the fays and fairy queen;
She played in wonderment upon the seat,
  And laughed, with laughing blossoms o'er her
    head;
She sat with daisies round about her feet,   .
  Till she was called to supper and to bed.

The seat in summer-tide was in the shade
      mingling boughs that swayed unto the
    ground,
And flecked the path, and pleasant music made;
  And bees were buzzing in the blooms around:
A maiden with a book of love-tales came,
  And read a sweet romance, to her all truth;
She closed the book, and whispered some one's
    name,
  Then went away to meet a favoured youth.

When misty autumn came, and currants hung
    In heavy, ripened clusters by the wall,
Chill winds came from the meadow-lands and
        swung
    The coloured trees that let their jewels fall :
Upon the seat a married couple stayed,
    With just a touch of care in their content ;
They watched the leaves that on the dry path
        played,
    Then arm-in-arm away they slowly went.

When winter came, and all the flow'rs were lost,
    And cold winds shrieked, and trees were black
        and bare,
The garden seat was whitened with the frost,
    And sparrows hopped in vain for crumbles there :
An old man came alone, with pale cheeks worn,
    And sat till night, and then he did not go ;
The snow fell with the dark, and in the morn
    The old man yet was there—still as the snow.

A DECEMBER DAISY.

LONE daisy dying in the winter wind,
  Did I not touch you in the early year?
Or was it one I may no longer find
    That graced the gay green where you now
    appear?
About dead leaves were hanging new blue-bells;
  The brook was singing in the wood, and oft
I heard the cuckoo call from distant dells
  To young birds learning carols in the croft.

But now old men, that in the summer day
  Sat sunning on the ale-bench by the wall,
Are shut indoors to nod dark hours away,
  And listen to the bits of snow that fall
Down the short cottage chimney. Summer's fire
  That warmed the heart is out; her flowers are
  lost,
And crushed with moorland moss to moorland
  mire,
  And burnt with coals or chilled to death with
  frost.

But you are left, though what were sighing trees
  Are now black fiends, and shake down ghostly
    songs
That withering winds bring from the winter seas,
  Where ships go down and mortals die in throngs.
Why are you here when all your mates are gone
  To that bright "londe of faery" whence they
    came?
Are you a failing and forgotten one
  That may not have a place nor yet a name?

It may be so, for I remember well
  You brought to mind a sweet and healthy child
When you were young; but now you seem to tell
  Of some poor girl forgotten and defiled.
When winds came lightly on you from the south,
  Your petals all were fresh from core to end,
And full of honey for the spoiler's mouth,
  But in your need you cannot gain a friend.

And why should I stand in the misty rain,
  And talk to you that cannot give reply?
Why should I with a sicken'd soul complain,
  Because a little daisy will not die?
The next cart-wheel that meets you with a groan
  May crush you to a grave beneath the rut;
Then why should I stand here and make a moan
  As though the senses of my eyes were shut?

It is because I may not lose the past,
 And quite forget the sweet things that have been ;
'Tis true the winter gloom has overcast
 The land, and blackened branches that were
  green ;
But I must still remember summer lanes,
 And think with thanks of birds that used to sing
And you are dearer, brighter for your stains,
 Amongst the happy mem'ries of the spring.

You cannot die, and you have not enough
 Of fairness left to tempt a truant hand
To pluck you from the daddock in the clough,
 And give your spirit to the summer land :
Come, I will free you from your prison tree,
 And for old days will bless you as I bow ;
When there is nothing left on earth for me
 May I be taken as I take you now.

PICTURES ON THE PANES.

How many pictures are there here,
  Upon the frozen panes this morn;
There is a river, broad and clear,
  And silver ships are on it borne.

And further on the palace-domes
  Of some bright elfin city shine;
And there are many stately homes
  Of merchants rich in wheat and wine.

Instead of coloured flow'rs of scent,
  The plants with diamonds are arrayed;
And trees with golden fruit are bent
  O'er garden walls of jewels made.

And far away, the fair clouds kiss
  The snowy tops of tor and hill—
Was ever picture like to this?
  Here is a real running rill!

And now the city, struck with fire,
  Is changed into a burning plain.
O ! what has made this mischief dire ?
  It is the sun upon the pane.

The hills themselves with fire are bound ;
  They slip, and on the city fall,
And crush it down into the ground,
  And there is ruin over all !

And now no palaces appear ;
  There is no city red with flame ;
Not anything of it is here—
  But water on the window-frame.

The meadows that indeed I see,
  In winter winds their joys have lost ;
But in the spring-time they will be
  Fairer than pictures in the frost.

SIMPLICITY.

With braided hair, a gentle girl,
    In hazel nook,
    Beside a brook
Flowing in many a playful twirl.

And by her side a bonny boy
    (Whose wooly breed
    At leisure feed)
Saith she may fill his years with joy.

No titles, gilded halls, or wealth,
    No marriage dower—
    A kiss, a flower,
No blessings save content and health.

Two children of forgotten race,
    When men were good,
    And woman's blood
The only colouring for her face.

How sweet to leave the noisy strife,
And dwell with thee,
Simplicity :
Love lasting and a quiet life !

WHILE THE SNOW FALLS.

WHILE the snow falls I can see
Pictures in my memory;
Many seasons they have lain
In some corner of the brain,
Covered up with meaner things
That our daily striving brings;
But this charm of mingling white
Has restored them to the light.
They before me are as plain
As the bow made in the rain
By the sun in summer days.

Many whitened winter ways
In a wind-blown town I see,
That in old days was to me
Happier than aught now can be.
That was ere this aged face
Had been furrowed in the race,
Had been worn by fight or fear,
Had but known the childish tear.

I can see myself in school,
Near the master on his stool ;
Snow is scrabbling on the pane,
Dancing all along the lane ;
It is hissing in the fire,
And it hides the old church spire :
Slowly, slowly fades the light,
Gently, strangely comes the night ;
This may not be much to see,
But it has a charm for me,
That would sooner wet my cheek,
Than the words that men can speak.

While the snow falls I can hear
Songs that made the old home dear ;
What shall ever come again
Like a mother's simple strain ?
What shall make the heart rejoice
Like a father's ringing voice ?
Years have gone by, one by one ;
Songs and singers too are gone ;
Time, who teaches us too late
What is good in our estate,
Comes in after years to show
What we let so lightly go,
When it is too late for blessing
Those who tired not in caressing.

While the snow falls—nay, no more,
Sorrowing will not joys restore;
Though of much we are bereft,
Still we all have something left.

THE LADY OF BLACK FRIARS.

THE trees all silent in the blue morn stood,
  And frosted leaves were lit with many lights
Of suns in miniature, when through the wood
    Rode first King James of Scotland and his
      knights :
Their hearts were bent upon a feast at Perth—
  A time to love a lady and be merry ;
And they were full of badinage and mirth,
  Until the white road took them to the ferry ;
Then laughter left them, for a woman came
With evil speech, and called the king by name.

She faced them all, and raised her bony hand,
  And lifted up her wan and wither'd face :
" My lord, the great King of the Northern Land,
  This ferry leads unto your burial-place !
Seek not for Charon and his boat of death,
  Nor laugh at my foreknowledge of the truth ;
Your life is but a thing of one day's breath,
  If you reck not the warning word of Ruth :

I am a prophetess, and know the sorrow
That may or may not come upon the morrow."

He laugh'd aloud, but in his heart was fear,
   For in a book of mystery he had read
A king in Scotland should be slain that year,
   And he bethought the year was nearly dead;
But how could he, in all his bravery,
   Confess before his knights in humble voice
That he had faith in woman's dreamery?—
   The king of power could not be king of choice;
And so he cross'd the river, and she stood
In silence watching them on Charon's flood.

*   *   *   *   *

The winter moon on sleeping thorps look'd down,
   And show'd the traveller distant halls and spires;
Keen frost went silently about the town,
   And silver'd o'er the Abbey of Black Friars.
Inside the abbey love danced in the halls,
   And firelight on fair faces threw its gloss;
Outside, where ivy on the aged walls
   Had written legends that were bound with moss,
A woman stood, a diddering sad thing,
Shut out because she went to warn the king.

" For well I know," she said, " that on this night
  Comes Graham from the mountains with his
    men ;
The king, because he does not heed the light,
  Shall never see the sun or me again."
The king had sent the prophetess away,
  And he was telling guests, with wine made merry,
How the mad crone had met him on that day,
  And dared him and his knights to cross the
    ferry ;
But ere he ended, hearts were struck with fear,
For noise of men in armour they could hear !

Then came the clash of swords in wild uproar,
  And torches flash'd the windows with red light ;
" Conceal the king, and double bolt the door,
  Till he has time to fit himself for flight ! "
The bolt was gone ! the men were hot in chase !
  Then Catherine Douglas ran to make or mar,
And with celestial beauty in her face
  Lifted her arm and placed it as a bar !
A moment more, and swords were through to
    wrench
The door, but she stood there and did not blench ;

Until her arm was broken, and she fell
  With pallid mouth aswoon upon the floor ;

And then rush'd in the ruthless hounds of hell,
  To make the feasting scene a scene of gore.
None thought of that brave lady who had done
  A deed full worthy of her Douglas blood.
December's dreary days were well-nigh run—
  The year was passing to oblivion's flood,
But ere it went out with the sobbing rain,
'Twas known a king in Scotland had been slain.

WE WILL HOLD OUR OWN.

WHILE there are men upon our British earth
Who love the Northern, free land of their birth,
  Throughout the world let it be known
  That we will guard and hold our own—
  That we will beat the same old bounds,
  Rememb'ring what are English grounds;
  Rememb'ring too what fields were stained
  With British blood ere they were gained.

    Shall we our fathers' work forget?
    No, let us hold their prizes yet!
    And, fighting only for the right,
    Keep England's name and honour bright.

The ewels of our honoured British crown
Were won by fighting sires of great renown,
  Who loved their homes but did not fear,
  To face the robber drawing near:
  They forfeited their ease and blood
  To keep the name of England good,
  And with their swords they made a way
  For rights we must uphold to day:

Shall we their giants' work forget ?
No, let us hold their prizes yet ;
And, fighting only for the right,
Keep England's name and honour bright.

Our fathers took the fields and faced the guns
Not for themselves alone, but for their sons ;
We must be worthy of their fame,
Or our own sons will blush for shame ;
So let it through the world be known
That we will surely hold our own,
And still be ready with our blood
To keep our fathers' honour good :

Shall we their giants' work forget ?
No, let us hold their prizes yet !
And fighting only for the right,
Keep England's name and honour bright.

CHASTELARD TO MARY STUART.

Dear heart, I bless you for this parting grace,
 That is as sunshine on a winter day ;
Now that last looks may be upon your face,
 There nothing is can wound me on my way ;
Filling my prison with a light divine,
 My queen, you come as does a saintly moon,
And I forget the dark clouds while you shine,
 And take no heed of that which will be soon.
Was ever fate like mine ? so dark and sweet ?
Love's feast before me, and I may not eat—

Love's feast, for I have won your heart at last,
 And may not tarry for a lover's kiss ;
But rich reward for future pain and past
 Is this one hour—this present hour of bliss.
What though another night shall find me dead,
 With no more sense of love and summer morn ?
I lived to put a crown upon my head
 That shall be with me in the time unborn ;

Nor may I be deceived with dying breath—
Speech is prophetic on the day of death.

Trust me, my perfect love, this midnight walk
    Is but a fretful prologue to the play—
Anxietude and doubt and troubled talk,
    Then writing shows the scene for Heaven-Day.
How tell you all in such a breathless time?
    When Death is standing with his door ajar,
Counting the minutes in a dreadful rhyme,
    Till he may take his whetted scythe, and mar
The glorious garden where my pleasures grew
To music and new hope because of you.

It is a fearful fall to truest knights—
    This headlong tumble to a mystic goal,
This slipping from God's sky and all its lights,
    To dirt and darkness in a narrow hole ;
But unto me an angel came to show
    That we imagine all the bitter part—
One crack of thunder and one seething glow
    Of lightning, and a little timid start,
And there an end ; the storm becomes a charm,
With promise of new life without alarm.

I do remember in Love's land of France,
    Whither best thoughts do truant-like run back,

Our life was zoned with light and fair romance,
   And dance and glamour followed in the track :
Nay, these are not poor flow'rs I pluck so late ;
   They have the scent of early love, and tho'
Some poison buds come too, they are of Fate,
   And honey were not sweet if 'twere not so.;
All is for love, and deadly nightshade grows
As much by Heaven's will as does the rose.

When that the gentle Hero held the light,
   Leander, knowing then her truth to him,
Sank under sea in his extreme delight,
   And in Life's river could no longer swim :
Now that you hold this loving light to me,
   Death's river, where the clouds hang in the night,
Shall be as glorious as Leander's sea,
   And the mysterious ferry shall be bright ;
Your tears are bitter-sweet, e'en I could weep
For joy of this " Good night, and pleasant sleep."

Stay your tears, my sweet, and no more speech
   Shall come from me of Death ; if my heart's
   kiss
Can cure your aphony, I do beseech
   Your lips a little, that I may not miss

The melody locked up with your dear voice.

This pure and precious time can no pain give,
But only gentle faith, and I rejoice

In knowledge of love strong enough to live :
Your hand is heaven, my love ; I feel your kiss ;
Your eyes speak peace, and now the rest is bliss.

THE FREE SWORD.

WHEN Peace sends fighters to the field,
  To guard the treasures of her land,
They do not go as slaves who yield
  Unto a despot king's command ;
Each man obeying her is free,
  And fights that freedom may abide ;
When duty calls him over sea,
  He takes a free sword by his side.

Fair Peace, who blesses art and trade,
  And crowns her working, worthy sons,
Must guard the Temple she has made,
  With fire and sword and " shotted guns ; "
Yea, Peace must her just works defend,
  And sometimes further make her way,
With any force that need may send,
  Till all men her commands obey.

What if the despots gain her ground ?
  Shall she bear olive in her hands ?

With slaughtered votaries around,
  And burning grain and bloody lands?
No, Peace shall take her great free blade,
  'Gainst which their strength shall be as straw,
And strike, till all men are afraid
  To bar her progress and her law.

WRITTEN IN BLOOD.

THE morning sun is shining on dry leaves
 That line the winter woods with faded fires ;
And the chill wind that for the summer grieves,
 Plays sad despairing tunes on frosted lyres.
Lord Langton he has won his love, and knows
 The joy that is reward for years of pain ;
And he is waiting till the darkness grows,
 And wishing it may come with wind and rain,
That they may steal away, and in black night
Find safety that will lead them to the light.

And still he walks in that dead forest hall,
 Where the nipped leaves have fallen from the
  roof
To lie about the cup-moss on the wall ;
 And there he tries to keep all fear aloof :
" Sir Stephen will be with her for a while,
 And she will give him his full share of sorrow :
Then in few minutes will my fortune smile,
 And we shall be away upon the morrow ;

I take a charm to make my burdens light—
A lady for whom all brave lords would fight."

The trees are still between two misty moons—
  One up in heaven and one in the stream,
And hung on dark dead boughs are snow festoons,
  And fairy chains with tiny stars agleam,
Lord Langton listens with his greedy ears ;
  He starts at night birds and the baying hounds,
And his sweet ague of fair hopes and fears
  Suggests strange meanings to mysterious sounds.
'Tis time ! he moves along the silent floor,
And—there is running blood beneath her door !

LOVE'S HARVEST.

LONG had I wandered in Circean lands,
   Where dreams of love are only dreams that pass,
And known the cruel kindness of white hands,
   And lips like lilies set in adder's grass:
True love came not, Marie; I turned aside,
   And strayed, and felt a cursed one as I stood,
Till you were with me as a gracious guide,
   And then I knew the world—that it is good.

Love's garden had erewhile begun to parch
   In thunder-heat, and no sweet rain to sing:
And I was fainting in my weary march—
   The day to me was but a deadly thing,
And night a terror: and the sun-heat grew;
   It choked green things with dust, and cracked
      the land;
And no rain fell on earth and no wind blew;
   Then, sinking, I was saved by your dear hand.

O 2

And then the coolness came, and drought was
    done,
And blessed showers of rain fell through the
    night,
With quiet hopeful music, till the sun
    Showed all my blossoms shining red and white :
You were my rainbow-love, the promise given,
    On that blue silent morning after rain,
That my new heart should not be sorely riven,
    Nor my new garden bent with blight again.

THE BETTER CHRISTMAS.

At length the long nights with their chilling rain
Have murmured in the Christmas-tide again,
And once more men are list'ning to the voice
That made the good men of old time rejoice—
That still will sanctify our lives, and cheer
The sick and sad who suffer through the year.

Ah ! much the name of Christ is at this time ;
More than the preacher's word—the poet's rhyme,
For these may not interpret what is known
Unto the spirit when the rose full blown
Makes our eyes dim with joy in early June—
It is beyond all sermon, song, or tune.

So is the thought of Christ beyond our speech—
Beyond the subtlety that song can reach ;
The little learned men too wise to know
May fret us, but the name of Christ shall grow ;
And His old teaching wond'ring men shall heed ;
There is no other light—it is their need.

And though we pray the less, may yet some deeds
Be better prayers for us than counting beads ;
About our hills, throughout our crowded land,
Great homes for poor and helpless people stand—
For orphans, for the sick, the halt, and old ;
Built in the unbelieving age of gold.

Because good work is done from east to west
We have the Better Christmas—not the best :
Still it shall grow to greater goodness yet ;
The words of Christ true men shall not forget ;
But knowing them the juster they shall be,
Whether to Him or not they bend the knee.

The right because of Him is still made strong,
And His name weakens yet the work of wrong ;
But wrong is with us still: we laugh aloud,
We feast and mingle with th' unthinking crowd ;
And there are men this moment lying dead
For want of human love, and help, and bread.

Is this not so ?   The children of the poor
Can smell your feast as they pass by the door ;
They are not seen—they are so small, they pass
Below the level of the window glass ;
They are not heard—they walk the frozen street
In silence, for they tread with shoeless feet.

You do not see nor hear, but you must know
That by your window now and then they go ;
Your pet dog has good meat upon his mat,
And warm and well fed is your sleeping cat ;
But poor bairns have not food, nor warmth, nor
  light :
You dare not think where they will sleep this
  night.

Why do we not remember ?   Let us share
A little, and enjoy our Christmas fare :
And now to all, who think or who forget,
May some new worth or happiness come yet ;
And may best thoughts, crowning the festal cheer,
Shape better lives to make the better year.

ZEPHADEE.

THE baron sat among his guests—
They drunk the ruby wine,
And ember light showed faces bright
And made the goblets shine.

Witch-cries rode rampant on the wind,
Down came the drenching rain;
The guests drank on, and every one
Filled full his cup again.

The baron had his daughter there—
She sat at his right hand,
And bosoms swelled when eyes beheld
The love of all the land.

Her face was as a lady-smock,
Red fainting in the white;
Ay, she was fair and debonnair—
Thrice worthy any knight.

No lips had ever won her heart,
Though lips had often said,
" Sweet Angeline, wilt thou be mine ? "
And she had turned her head.

Now while loud laughter drowned the jest,
And brown beer drowned despight,
A minstrel came in Jesus' name
For shelter from the night.

" What is thy name ? " the baron said ;
" A minstrel seemest thou ;
An thou dost bring a song to sing,
Thou shalt be served, I trow."

" Good master of the festal throng,
I come from Paynim strand,
And I will sing of our brave king
Who fights in Holyland."

" What is thy name ? " the baron cried,
" I come from far-off strand,"
" Now, fire and flame, what is thy name ? "
" I come from Fairyland."

Fierce anger lit the baron's brow ;
He shouted sword in hand,

With scoffing breath, " Take him to death !
  He comes from Fairyland."

The minstrel moved nor eye nor limb,
  But said as he did stand,
" Drop down thy sword upon the board :
  I come from Fairyland."

" Take him to death ! " the baron cried.
  The minstrel one word spake :
Down dropped the sword upon the board,
  And all but one did quake.

Then joy was in the minstrel's eye ;
  " Come hither, Angeline ;
My name to thee is *Zephadee* ;
  I would that thou wert mine.

" For I have searched through Fairyland
  For one as fair as thee,
And none but thou, and this I vow,
  Hath charmèd *Zephadee*."

She looked into his face and saw
  The lover of her dreams :
" Yea, I am thine, thy Angeline,
  Thou lover of my dreams.

" I knew that thou wouldst come for me
  In sweet love-land to roam,
Where fairies play by night and day
  About thy palace home."

The guests were bounden by a spell ;
  They could not laugh nor frown ;
If one held up a brimming cup
  He could not lay it down.

The minstrel turned him to the guests,
  And took away the charm :
" I came not here to bring ye fear,
  Or work ye any harm.

" I came to seek a maïden's smile,
  And find my wonder joy—
Fair Angeline for aye is mine,
  And our love may not cloy.

" Now let the wine go round again,
  And to this festal band
I straight will tell what thing befell
  That won me Fairyland.

" I journeyed long from Palestine,
  And came to Britain's shore ;

(Sit, love, by me, thy Zephadee,
  And I will tell thee more.)

" I sang of deeds in Holyland—
  I sang of Richard's fame,
And by the sea there came to me
  A grey man, old and lame.

" That old grey-bearded man came close,
  And took me by the hand :
' Wilt sing again to me that strain,
  And win thee Fairyland ?'

" I laughed because his words seemed
      strange,
  And laughing loosed his hand :
I sang again to him that strain,
  And won me Fairyland.

" Give me thy child, and I will give
  Whate'er thou mayst demand ;
At dawn of day we'll sail away
  Unto the Summer land.

" There all that is, is surely best ;
  There love is love indeed ;
And care is not in that fair spot,
  And sorrows do not bleed.

" All that are in the isle of bliss,
    Delight in every day.
Ah ! ye who tread in daily dread
    Know not how blest are they."

The baron his young daughter gave
    Unto that stranger guest,
" And now," said he, " give thou to me
    The thing that is the best."

" When shines the full moon on the earth,
    Shall be what is the best :
Sweet Angeline, now thou art mine,
    And joy is with my quest."

Proud Zephadee and Angeline
    Watched for the lagging day ;
The morning came with sun aflame,
    And gold was on the hay.

A rosy bark with silken sails
    Danced lightly in the wind ;
The lovers two went o'er the blue,
    And left the land behind.

Upon the castle's battlements,
    The baron's guests did stand,

And watched them glide upon the tide
Away to Fairyland.

Away! away! in the golden morn!
Towards the west away!
The bark swept on and they were gone
For ever and for aye!

The baron waited for the moon,
The full moon in the sky;
The sun set thrice, and then his eyes
Beheld the moon on high.

He looked thereon with anxious face,
Now! now he would be blest!
He fell away from dark and day,
For death it is the best.

WILDERMERE.

Sir Ivan sat beside his love,
  Under a beechen tree ;
The wood was all aglow with bloom,
  And all aglow was he,
For that young maid to him had said
  That she his wife would be.

There came a bearded woman by—
    A woman foul to see ;
The dog she had was gaunt and grim,
  And gaunt and grim was she ;
She shook her staff and laughed the laugh
  Of fiendish villainy.

" I know thee," said that grisly dame,
  " And I will spoil your cheer ;
I came unto your door for food
  In winter-time last year ;
You drove me thence, sans food or pence,
  Sir Ivan Wildermere."

" I knew thee for a witch," he said,
  " Thou didst not come to me
As women come who starve for food,
  And cold and hungry be—
Thou didst not shrink for meat or drink,
  Thou hateful prodigy."

The beldame stared with ghostly eye,
  And came to where they sat ;
The dog growled and his mistress growled,
  And at the lovers spat :
" Sir Wildermere, see what is here,
  Thy trothplight is a cat."

Sir Wildermere looked with a blench
  On her he should affy,
And lo ! she was a four-legged thing,
  And set her back up high :
She wagged a long tail, and the hag
  Laughed at him devilishly.

Then spake she unto Wildermere,
  . " This dog I have with me
Was once a knight, and thou mayhap
  Some day a dog wilt be :
Come cat and dog, now we must jog,
  Good morrow bellamy."

Sir Ivan sank down alamort,
    A sad astonied knight,
For his belovèd Marian
    He had no power to fight ;
As good essay to dim the day,
    Or make the darkness bright.

Night lit her lamps, and pale despair
    Laid Ivan in a swoon ;
He dreamt of love that was alate
    Under the white-faced moon—
The roses wept, and Ivan slept
    The sleep that is a boon.

The sun shone slanting in the morn
    Through matted folds of may,
The eglantine dropped spangle-beads
    Before him as he lay ;
And on the knight played amber light,
    He woke, and it was day !

He looked around him with a smile,
    And left his leafy lair,
" Now is my heart as full of joy
    As it was full of care,
For now I know which way to go,
    Aad fate again is fair.

P

" Though devils bring the spite of hell
    To blight a mortal's weal,
For every sore there is a salve
    So long as hearts are leal,
And sleep hath sent medicament
    My poison-wound to heal."

He went away by stream and lake
    That lay as smooth as glass,
By blossom bough and tangle-wood
    That sighed as he did pass ;
And in between was gold and green
    Of buttercups and grass.

Still on he went until he came
    Unto a dreary dell
That made a stench, and all around
    Was dim and dank as hell ;
And in that spot there stood a cot,
    And there the witch did swell.

He strode up to that danger cot,
    Of scorn and anger full,
And saw about the house leg-bones
    And on each bone a skull,
And white and lone 'mong bleaching bone
    Blew roses beautiful.

The wily witch grinned at the door,
  And picked a human bone ;
" I come to kill thine evil craft,
  And make thee to atone ;
I fear no harm, I bear a charm
  More potent than thine own."

And therewithal his shining blade,
  From out the sheath he drew ;
The witch stood up, and in a trice
  Her iron nose she blew
In trumpet sound, and from the ground
  Two giant things upgrew.

" I do not fear ye," said the knight,
  " Nor Doubt, nor yet Despair ; "
A bogglish light was in their eyes
  That looked in devil stare—
He fought the two and both he slew,
  The dame died with a blare.

He took his love from under ban,
  After the deadly fight ;
Then tapped he upon every skull,
  And each became a knight ;
And by his side each hath his bride
  From scented roses white.

And joy was unto every knight,
   For dead were Doubt and Fear ;
And joy was unto ev'ry maid
   For many a merry year—
And more than all the joy did fall
   To Ivan Wildermere.

EDGAR.

AFTER long errant strife abroad,
  Lord Danion homeward came,
To eat and drink awhile in peace,
  And win love by his fame.

As he rode inland with his squire,
  Smiles on his dark face played,
For in the land of home and love
  All sounds sweet music made.

At farmsteads Saxon men would scowl,
  As passed the Norman Knight;
But he would laugh fair greeting back,
  For his young heart was light;

And he cared not what men might be,
  Or whether they looked grim,
So long as he had share of wealth,
  And harm came not to him.

Two years ere this he sought to win
　Elfa, a Saxon maid,
Whose father, Egbert, yet had wealth
　After each Norman raid.

Lord Danion had for rival then
　Edgar, a Saxon youth ;
But Danion wooed with more of craft,
　Though not with more of truth.

He won the father, but the maid
　Looked on his love as guile ;
And all his kindness and his vows
　Could not make Elfa smile.

Edgar could only say he loved,
　Still Elfa soon he won ;
But Egbert gave to him no hope
　That he might be his son.

At length the father counselled them
　That each should go his way,
And join some lord in fray and feud,
　For two years and a day.

The one who won the most of fame,
　Should win the most of love ;
And he would take him for his son,
　Upon his word and glove.

And now from sea, by chilly moor,
  By wood and battlement,
Lord Danion with an old squire rode,
  And his thoughts loveward went.

" Peter, dost thou not think it well,"
  He said, with slack'ning rein,
" To be with English birds and trees,
  In the old land again ?

" Some idling days, with simple sport,
  Will not befall amiss,
After rough times of bloody work,
  Nor will a maiden's kiss."

" Ay, it is well to leave the fight,
  With its grim daily threat,
And think that Death, a long way off,
  Will seek not for us yet ;

" Till long, long summers we have had
  With feasts in gay attire ;
Till long, long winters we have sat
  With loved ones by the fire.

" That he will leave us to this life,
  Till we with age are white,
Then kindly come as our best friend,
  To guide us through the night."

" But surely, Peter, thou dost not
 Look forward to thy prime,
But rather backward, for thine age
 Is in its autumn-time ?"

" And may not my gold autumn be
 As long as thy green spring ?
And my fruit satisfy as much
 As when thy love-birds sing ?

" How blessed are the peaceful men
 Who fear nor age nor death,
Who gently live, and in the end
 With smiles can yield their breath !

" And how deceived are men who seek
 For quarrels stained with blood !
And call their broil their honour's fight,
 That some may think it good.

" Who for no cause, but their own pride,
 Will put in flames a town,
And make the children fatherless
 For glorious renown !

" Their deeds of blood shall stain their souls,
 Till they bend under years,
And people all their guilty ways
 With fiends and crowds of fears."

" Now art thou not a strange old squire
    To follow a young knight,
Whose love and honour must be won
    In camp, and field, and fight ?

" Thou speakest plainly to thy lord,
    Now will I speak to thee :
In this day's journey 'twixt us two,
    There need no quarrel be ;

" And when we come to Egbert's Hall
    At Withold, thou mayst go ;
I know but little of thee now,
    And little wish to know.

" Our battles bring strange men to fight,
    And some strange men to serve ;
And I have given place to thee
    That thou didst not deserve."

Then Peter, " Shall I not have rest ?
    Do not my old limbs tire ?
What shall I do when thou dost take
    Thy full cup by the fire ? "

" If thou dost wish for shelter there
    It shall be giv'n to thee ;
And if thou keep a quiet tongue,
    Thou shalt have fare with me.

"It will be better so for thee,
    And better so for me;
For as my quest is one of love,
    I wish for harmony;

"In turn, be civil for the night;
    Chime in with no rude chord;
And in the morning thou mayst seek
    New venture and new lord."

So rode they, and few words were said;
    And nought strange did befall:
At eve the young lord blew his horn
    Before old Withold Hall.

The gate was passed, and Egbert's folk
    Made merry for their guest;
For tidings did not often come
    To them from east or west.

And now there would be much ado;
    Great feasting in the hall;
Tales from the wars; with perhaps at end,
    A marriage festival:

Then would they have good cheer enough
    For any king or queen;
And don new caps, with ribbons fine,
    For games upon the green.

After the feast Lord Danion talked,
  With folk agape to hear,
Of deeds that he had done in fight,
  With trusty sword and spear.

Fair Elfa was in wonderment,
  And yet she heard in gloom ;
And sat so still she seemed to be
  Like to a flow'r in bloom.

Her gentle face gave dreams of hope,
  As does the blessed morn
In the blue summer ; and her hair
  Was as the sunlit corn.

Then Danion, in a vengeful mood,
  Told with loud scoffing breath,
How Edgar in the battle fell,
  And died a coward's death :

How he grew pale with recreant fear,
  And turned away from fight,
And was o'ertaken by a boy,
  And slain in his base flight.

Then Elfa bent her fair young head,
  And her clasped hands became
Wet with her tears ; and Egbert's heart
  Stood still for Saxon shame :

With hatred for the Norman host
  His blood within ran wild;
But he must show them courtesy
  For home and for his child.

Old Peter on the darken'd ground
  Was lying all alone;
He was not minded by the guests,
  Nor seen by anyone.

In this sad pause he spoke, " The lord
  In battles great hath been;
And now, good host, I pray you hear
  What this old man hath seen.

" I am a Saxon; there are few
  Who know, and fewer care;
And I have nothing left to lose,
  So I can speak out fair.

" 'Tis true the Saxon Edgar fell,
  But it was not in flight:
Nor was it in the light of day,
  But in the dark still night.

" Three murd'rers took him in his sleep,
  And I have heard men say
The Norman hound who set them on
  Shall yet be brought to bay."

(When Danion heard these words he laughed,
  But in his soul was fear;
His face was blanched, but turned from light
  It did not so appear.)

" Edgar fought well, but won no fame,
  'Tis not now Saxon food."
(Egbert, remembering his wrongs,
  Showed in his face his blood.)

" While Saxon sires can hardly keep
  Together land and name,
Why should they think that Norman tongues
  Will to their sons give fame?

" Believe me, lady, I have seen
  Thy love fight this same lord,
And he has so belaboured him
  That he could speak no word."

" Who is it says so to my face?"
  Cried Danion in his scorn;
" Why thou hast been my serving-man,
  Thou slave of those mean born!"

" What then? Did I not serve thee well?
  As well as age may youth?
And dost thou think when men grow old
  They dare not speak the truth?

"I only say the thing I know,
  And saw with mine own eyes ;
Therefore the truth is not with thee,
  And thy strange tales are lies."

Then Danion sprang unto his feet
  To answer with a blow,
But Egbert grasped him by the arm,
  And would not let him go.

As Elfa shrank away for fear,
  The old man laughed and said,
"I pray thee do not let him harm
  This serving-man's white head."

And Danion then, "Thou mocking slave,
  Yet will I hold my rage ;
Thy sense is leaving thee, and thou
  Art foolish in thine age."

"No more, no more—let quarrel end,"
  Said the good Egbert then ;
"No more of Norman or Saxon ;
  Come drink as mortal men."

But Danion, growling yet awhile,
  The board struck with his hand,
And said, "No man that I have met
  Can my good sword withstand."

Old Peter, coming from the dark,
  And standing in the glow,
Said, with a smile, " Behold, Sir Liar,
  The man who can do so."

Then Danion fell back with a cry!
  Amazed the guests did stare!
For it was no old man came forth,
  But Edgar who stood there!

" O rest thee, rest thee, in the grave !
  O rest thee with the dead !
O mercy, mercy!" Danion cried,
  " Thy blood is on my head!"

" Indeed I hope that I may rest,
  Though not yet in my grave,
But with my love, and thou mayst yet
  Live well and thy soul save.

" I am no ghost : I was struck down,
  But I got up again ;
And with the three men did contend,
  Till two of them were slain :

" The third, I held him by the throat,
  For mercy he did crave ;
And he confessed what I have said,
  That he his life might save.

" I let him live, and made him swear,
　As his soul might be free,
That he should tell thee I was dead,
　Then in a task aid me.

" For well he knew, as thou dost know,
　If false I had him found,
I could have grasped him in my arms,
　And thrown him dead to ground.

" Did he not speak to thee of one,
　Though old, who had strange power
Of telling signs, and healing wounds,
　And sores, by herb and flower ?

" Did he not say that this old man
　O'er English ground could guide,
And serve thee well in camp and field,
　And many ways beside ?

" And so disguised I sought and served,
　With thee from place to place,
That some day I might tell this tale,
　In this Hall to thy face."

Then Edgar unto Elfa turned,
　And lovers' doubts were done,
For Egbert to the Saxon came,
　And blessed him as his son.

Lord Danion left the Hall that night,
Alone in rain and wind ;
And Edgar, filling full his cup,
With Elfa stayed behind.

THE END.

www.ingramcontent.com/pod-product-compliance
Lightning Source LLC
Chambersburg PA
CBHW030103030726
47498CB00007B/2235